GRASPING
MYSTERIES

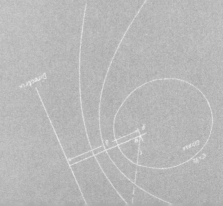

$$r = \frac{p}{1 + \epsilon \cos \theta}$$

$$p = r_i \left(v_i/v_s\right)^2 \cos^2 \gamma_i$$

$$\tan \theta_i = \tan \gamma_i \left[\frac{p/r_i}{p/r_i - 1}\right]$$

$$\epsilon = \frac{1}{\cos \theta_i} \left[\frac{p}{r_i} - 1\right]$$

$$\text{when } \gamma_i = 0, \ \epsilon = \left|\left(v_i/v_s\right)^2 - 1\right|$$

GRASPING MYSTERIES
Girls Who Loved Math

JEANNINE ATKINS

ATHENEUM BOOKS FOR YOUNG READERS
New York London Toronto Sydney New Delhi

 ATHENEUM BOOKS FOR YOUNG READERS

An imprint of Simon & Schuster Children's Publishing Division

1230 Avenue of the Americas, New York, New York 10020

Text copyright © 2020 by Jeannine Atkins

Illustrations copyright © 2020 by Victoria Assanelli

ATHENEUM BOOKS FOR YOUNG READERS is a registered trademark of Simon & Schuster, Inc. Atheneum logo is a trademark of Simon & Schuster, Inc.

For information about special discounts for bulk purchases, please contact Simon & Schuster Special Sales at 1-866-506-1949 or business@simonandschuster.com.

The Simon & Schuster Speakers Bureau can bring authors to your live event. For more information or to book an event, contact the Simon & Schuster Speakers Bureau at 1-866-248-3049 or visit our website at www.simonspeakers.com.

Book design by Debra Sfetsios-Conover and Irene Metaxatos

The text for this book was set in Old Claude STD.

The illustrations for this book were rendered in pencil, then worked digitally.

Manufactured in the United States of America

0620 BVG

First Edition

10 9 8 7 6 5 4 3 2 1

Library of Congress Cataloging-in-Publication Data

Names: Atkins, Jeannine, 1953– author.

Title: Grasping mysteries : girls who loved math / Jeannine Atkins.

Description: First edition. | New York City : Atheneum Books for Young Readers, [2020] | Audience: Ages 10 Up. | Audience: Grades 4–6. | Summary: A biographical novel in verse of seven girls from different time periods who used math to explore the mysteries of the universe and grew up to do innovative work that changed history.

Identifiers: LCCN 2019037196 | ISBN 9781534460683 (hardcover) | ISBN 9781534460706 (eBook)

Subjects: LCSH: Herschel, Caroline Lucretia, 1750–1848—Childhood and youth—Juvenile fiction. | Nightingale, Florence, 1820–1910—Childhood and youth—Juvenile fiction. | Ayrton, Hertha, 1854–1923—Childhood and youth—Juvenile fiction. | Tharp, Marie—Childhood and youth—Juvenile fiction. | Johnson, Katherine G.—Childhood and youth—Juvenile fiction. | Paisano, Edna L.—Childhood and youth—Juvenile fiction. | Rubin, Vera C., 1928–2016—Childhood and youth—Juvenile fiction. | CYAC: Novels in verse. | Herschel, Caroline Lucretia, 1750–1848—Childhood and youth—Fiction. | Nightingale, Florence, 1820–1910—Childhood and youth—Fiction. | Ayrton, Hertha, 1854–1923—Childhood and youth—Fiction. | Tharp, Marie—Childhood and youth—Fiction. | Johnson, Katherine G., 1918–2020—Childhood and youth—Fiction. | Paisano, Edna L., 1948–2014—Childhood and youth—Fiction. | Rubin, Vera C., 1928–2016—Childhood and youth—Fiction. | Mathematicians—Fiction. | Scientists—Fiction. | Sex role—Fiction.

Classification: LCC PZ7.5.A85 Gr 2020 | DDC [Fic]—dc23

LC record available at https://lccn.loc.gov/2019037196

TO PETER LAIRD,
AGAIN AND ALWAYS

GRASPING
MYSTERIES

CONTENTS

LOOKING UP

Caroline Herschel (1750–1848) was the first woman to discover a comet, to earn a salary for scientific research, and to win a gold medal from the Royal Astronomical Society in England.

MAKING CHANGE WITH CHARTS, PART I

Florence Nightingale (1820–1910) was a trailblazing nurse and statistician whose work reformed hospitals.

EXPLORING CURRENTS

Hertha Marks Ayrton (1854–1923) graduated as a math major from one of the first colleges open to women and became an electrical engineer and inventor.

MAPPING WHAT'S HIDDEN

Marie Tharp (1920–2006) studied math and geology in college and graduate school, then mapped the ocean floor.

CREATING PATHS THROUGH SPACE

Katherine Johnson (1918–2020) graduated from college as a math major, then charted courses around the earth and to the moon for NASA astronauts.

MAKING CHANGE WITH CHARTS, PART II

Edna Lee Paisano (1948–2014) was the first Native American statistician to work full-time at the US Census Bureau.

LOOKING BEYOND

Vera Rubin (1928–2016) found strong evidence for the existence of dark matter, opening up new questions about the universe. She became the second woman to win a gold medal from the Royal Astronomical Society.

Behind the Verse: A Note from the Author

Women Who Widened Horizons

Selected Bibliography

LOOKING UP

✦

CAROLINE HERSCHEL

(1750–1848)

The Promise

Fever blurs night and day, sense and nonsense.
Caroline can't tell the night watchman's call
from the chime of the postman's handbell.
She can't see far past the fog under her eyelids.
She feels hot, but craves more covers,
struggles to sip from a cup held to her mouth.
Water feels as coarse to swallow as sand.

One night she sees straight again
and wobbles to the window.
Star shine casts hope, reminds her
that smallpox didn't kill her when she was small.
Neither will typhus now.
She raises her arms as if she might touch the faraway.

Counting Notes

When Caroline is well enough to fetch butter and eggs
at the marketplace, Mama hands her a basket,
then ties a scarf over her face.
Cover your smallpox scars so no one stares.

The veil makes Caroline feel small,
the way she does when Mama says, *Don't be vain.*
Mama also warns, *Thou shall not covet,*
which means: *Don't want too much.*
She says Caroline has no need for music,
since a girl can't join a military band
like her father and older brothers.

But when Caroline bends over washtubs,
she sings. Papa, who's become too ill to march,
slips into the scullery with a violin. He shows her
how to tilt her chin and wrist so the bow's
particular angles pull music from just four strings.

A Girl's Education

Mama, who never learned to read and write,
says that with Caroline now twelve,
it's time to stop school. *If your father hadn't spoiled*
your brothers with so much education,
they might have kept closer to home.
You can be a help in the house and be thankful
you don't have to find work outside as a maid.
We're poor and you're plain, so you should expect little of life.

Mystery

The night sky is brighter than the fire in the hearth
where Caroline stirs mutton broth and roasts apples.
She smells medicine on her father's breath
as they step out to stand on cobblestones.
He tugs off the cloth that hides
her pockmarks, though it never covers her eyes.
He shows her how to hold up her hand
and spread her fingers to measure the spaces between stars.
There's more above than the moon and stars, Papa says
as a veil of shine disappears in the dark.

The kitchen door opens. Mama calls,
Caroline, no lady ever goes out without a hat.
Come inside. Night is dangerous.
She scolds Papa, *No wonder you're sick.*

You'll be fine, Papa whispers to Caroline.
As they head inside, they hum a song
meant to keep soldiers' steps steady.
Soon his sickness, not hers, fills the house.
But she never feels warm. Her mouth feels like moss.

After the Funeral

Caroline is seventeen when she packs
her father's old clothes, sells his trumpet and violin,
puts away his military ribbons and star almanac.
William, who's twelve years older than Caroline,
returns from England, asks, *Lina, do you still sing?*

Caroline can almost taste the question's sweetness.
She trills one of their father's favorite tunes.
When she's done, William says, *You'll need to learn*
some hymns and oratorios, but with training,
your voice could carry higher notes. He turns
to their mother. *She could come live with me*
in England and join the choir I conduct.

Mama shakes her head. *I'm a poor widow*
now and need her to keep house.

I'll send money so you can hire help,
William says. *If she shows no gifts*
after two Easter seasons, I'll send her back.

Caroline keeps her head down, tugging,
twisting, and crossing strands of cotton,
counting stitches, knitting enough stockings to last
her mother two years. She won't promise
to send more, lest her mother say she's vain
for hoping her voice is strong enough for her to stay.

The Journey

Caroline and William climb onto the roof
of a mail coach, which they ride for six days and nights.
They clutch each other as the horses whinny and swerve.
In Holland, wind sweeps Caroline's hat into a canal.
She and William board a crowded ship
and catch sleep
while standing on the deck.
Darkness and stars flicker above.

The next afternoon, clouds gather. Wild waves
pound the ship's sides. Men climb over rigging,
taking in sails. A gale splits a spar in two,
then snaps the main mast. As the deck floods,
sailors toss Caroline and William
onto the backs of two men in a lifeboat.
They're rowed to shore and hire a carriage.
The horses bolt and throw them into a ditch.

I shouldn't have brought you, William says.
Caroline brushes dirt off his jacket and her skirt.
They climb back to the road, catch a night coach

in London, and arrive in Bath early the next afternoon.
Walking down stone streets, William points out tearooms,
ballrooms, and concert halls. *Aristocrats come here*
on holiday to play cards, waltz, or take the waters.

Caroline can't make out much English,
but nods as gentlemen bedecked in elaborate wigs
and ladies in elegant gowns greet William.
Their glances at her seem friendly,
though her face is scarred and she doesn't wear a hat.

At William's house, she carries a candle
up the narrow stairs to an attic room.
She murmurs her evening prayers,
gets into her nightgown, then tumbles
onto the straw mattress, glad to lie down
after twelve days without a bed.
Still, they might be the happiest days of her life.

Practicing
BATH, ENGLAND

Caroline straightens sky maps stacked
on the harpsichord. She dusts a telescope
that William says makes the sky seem close.
It costs dearly, but an unmarried man
can afford to indulge his curiosity.
Sometime I'll show you how to use it.

Caroline shines William's shoe buckles,
cuts out ruffles for his shirts, sings
musical scales shaped by mathematics and air.
Every morning, she sets out coffee, rolls,
and currant jelly for William, who speaks
to her less in German and more in English.
She practices new words in the marketplace,
but mostly points as she chooses cherries and cider,
selects beef from the butcher. The new language
feels dense as a forest with no way out.
All the trees look alike.

But by winter, instead of *Kohl*, she says "cabbage,"
asks for "sausage" instead of *Wurst*.

She sings entirely in English, breathing deep
into her belly, finding sounds that skim the ceiling.
She aims for the sky, which every night
reminds her that what looks small is truly grand.

After Dark

William gives Caroline a turn at the telescope.
Stars spill into pale blue, rose, and yellow pools of light.
She swallows as if she might choke on a song.
What was always in the sky looks bigger,
making her want to see even more,
though she mustn't seem greedy,
as if she dared take a second spoonful of jam.

She steps back. *How big is the sky?*

No one knows, but we get a sense of the size
of the universe by measuring the distance
to Saturn, the farthest planet from Earth. See it?

Caroline again looks through the circle of glass.
Those gold rings! Her gaze shifts to the moon,
almost round as a face tonight, pockmarked,
like hers. *Could someone live on the moon?*

I think so. A telescope with wider mirrors
could reflect more details of its mountains

and craters, maybe signs of cities.
The longer you look, the more you see.
Even comets, which are bright as stars
but leave a spill of shine as they move.

I might have seen one long ago with Papa.
She keeps her eyes on the sky. I'd like to see another.

What's truly extraordinary is to be the first to spot one.
There's a lot no one has witnessed, which is why
we need stronger telescopes. They cost a lot,
but I've been reading about how to make them.

Caroline offers to help.

Reflections

William grinds glass for mirrors meant to catch starlight.
Caroline stirs in copper, tin, and different kinds of earth.
They heat the mixture, then pour it into a mold
to form a mirror that's slightly curved, like an eye.

William polishes the surface smooth with sand,
his hand circling for hour after hour,
a practice in patience and precision.
Lifting his fingertips even a moment
could make the metal harden and blur the shine.
Caroline sings or reads aloud so he won't be bored.
When he's thirsty or hungry, she holds a china cup
of tea or triangles of toast to his mouth.

At last they set the mirror in the base of a tube
carved from the heartwood used for oboes.
Darkness hides much on earth but hints
at what's lost in daylight. Night isn't a veil, but a door.

Hats

William shows Caroline how to balance
the household accounts. She adds the money
he receives for conducting and teaching music,
and now making telescopes to sell. She subtracts
what they spend and sends some to their mother.
There's not enough, so she folds and stitches
lace, silk, and velvet into hats.
She measures the circumference of a head,
cuts a diagonal line across felt, and calculates brims.
She sets hats for sale on the windowsill facing the street.

For the first time in her life, she has money
of her own. She reminds herself it's vain
to want more than her mother had.

Lost

Walking to the marketplace, Caroline passes women
wearing white caps and aprons who sit on doorsteps,
doing needlework beside babies dozing in baskets.
She could watch a sleeping infant for as long as a star,
wishes she could hold one,
though perhaps not the noisy kind.

Back in the quiet kitchen, she does division,
measures half a handful of flour, a pinch of salt,
gauging the depth of a pan to determine
how far she should keep it from the flames.

At supper, William teaches her more mathematics
so she can check his celestial calculations.
Spherical trigonometry is familiar from shifting yarn
with wrists and fingers, multiplying stitches of stockings,
subtracting to make room for the curves of heels and ankles.
But logarithms, which let multiplication and addition
switch places, make her feel as lost in a forest
as when English words first loomed around her.
William begins where many teachers end,
pushing so she's caught in thickets and thorns.

Dear Mother

Caroline dutifully writes letters she includes
with the money she posts to their mother each month.
A neighbor may or may not read aloud
Caroline's account of how she's useful to William,
copying music and star catalogs,
which list stars he's located and numbered,
so others might find what he saw in the night sky.

He now asks her to teach singers in the choir
he conducts. The tuition goes to him.
That seems fair. She doesn't write to her mother
that she was invited to perform in another city,
offered a regular salary. Of course she refused,
saying she'll sing only in choirs or when William conducts
in concert halls where women swat down skirts
that could fill seats of their own.
There Caroline's voice wavers, scoops up certainty.
She looks out at gentlemen wearing powdered wigs
who angle their necks to peer past ladies' towering hats.
She loves the short silence before her voice rises
with a song about a star over a manger,

which wise astronomers followed. She pushes
her voice past breath. *Lift up your heads.*

After four years in England, Caroline sings a solo.
Rejoice. One note reaches
for another as her voice fills a hall.

Minding the Heavens

On clear evenings, after supper and singing,
Caroline and William bring the telescope to the garden.
I'm charting double stars to learn if stars move.
William points out a pair of stars, one slightly above
the other. *I measure the distance between*
them to see if the gap changes over time.

He dips his head back to the eyepiece, then steps away.
He rubs his face as he records numbers in a ledger.
There's too much to remember, but if I write down everything,
I lose time waiting for my eyes to adjust from looking
close at paper, then back into the dark.

I could take notes so your gaze never
has to leave the sky, Caroline offers.

Soon she sits beside the telescope at a table
with a notebook and a lantern veiled
so its light doesn't dim William's view.
She charts what's known in the sky, dipping a quill in ink,
recording the sizes, colors, and locations of stars
on paper that turns a brighter white as the sun rises.

The Astronomer's Assistant

After breakfast, Caroline copies numbers,
keeping them strict and straight as a broomstick.
She classifies the shine and scale of stars,
plans the next night's schedule, including where
to aim the telescope, at what angle, and for how long.
She sharpens the tip of her quill,
then keeps her grip steady while drawing lines
down and across for boxes like tiny window frames.
They stand for sections of the vast sky to be examined.
She puts crosses in the parts seen.
Lines, slanted like her knitting needle to pluck yarn,
mark quadrants that call for another look.

William teaches her to create equations that hint
at when celestial objects might move in or out of sight.
Once-dependable numbers split, swell, surprise.
With practice, mathematics becomes less like a forest
and more like a clearing, the way English words
have become as familiar as the particular shapes
of a towering oak, bowing birches, junipers,
and the prickle of hawthorn branches or holly leaves.
Why had she ever thought these trees looked alike?

Beyond
BATH, ENGLAND, 1781

Most double stars are so far away that Caroline
can't distinguish the distance between them.
But with a telescope, what first looked like one star
sometimes shows itself as two, orbiting each other!

William spots and Caroline records dozens
of double stars, enough to suggest that many stars
come in pairs and that stars *do* move. The sky
is not a flat field decorated with constellations,
but more like an ocean with depths.

One night William spots a glimmer never reported.
As nights and weeks pass, its motion
in relation to surroundings suggests it's not a star.
He says, *Comets flash in and out of sight,
but there's no skirt of light trailing this orb.*
Night after night, he tracks the way it comes and goes
from view, measures its distance from earth
until he's certain he has found a planet never before seen.

Caroline works out equations that show
it may be twice as far from earth as Saturn.
If space holds room for another planet,
the universe must be like a blanket that keeps
unfolding, far larger than anyone thought.

Moving

Word of the new planet spreads with shock,
arguments, and finally joy. Learned men
from the Royal Astronomical Society visiting.
They ask William to come to London
to accept a gold medal. William wants to name
the planet in honor of King George III,
who sends congratulations and invites him to the palace.

When William returns, he tells Caroline
it was decided to keep to the tradition of taking
planets' names from mythology.
Uranus honors the muse of astronomy. *His Majesty*
offered me a salary to continue my observations
and show the wonders above to royalty and their guests,
he says. *We must move closer to Windsor Castle.*

William rents a house with a leaky roof near a river
that seems to make him ill, though he rubs his face
and hands with onions to prevent night fever.
He and Caroline move again to a big house in Slough.
He shows her around the old stables, says, *We can turn*
these into workrooms to make telescopes to sell.

It's awfully far from the village. As they walk into the house,
Caroline remembers the sound of her singing blending
with others, and may the good Lord forgive her,
applause, compliments, and making money.

The landlady said we might borrow a horse.

Caroline looks from the brother she loves
to the floors covered with dried and rotting leaves,
the windows blackened with soot. Housekeeping
looks endless, but she starts by sweeping ashes
from the hearth, taking flint from the tinderbox.
She strikes it on steel, fans the sparks.

Night Watches

Winter offers long nights with more time
to sweep the sky, moving the telescope like a broom
meant to gather every star. Standing on a platform
on a ladder by the tall telescope, William calls out numbers
to Caroline, who sits at a desk set on the ground below.
She tips a candle to melt ink in a bottle, writes down
distances and angles in relation to the North Pole.
Her toes feel frozen even padded
in fourteen pairs of stockings
under layers of flannel petticoats and wool skirts.
William won't take his eyes off the sky,
so she feeds him brown bread and cheese.

Names

They aren't as alone as she expected in the house far
from the main roads. Their landlady, a wealthy widow,
often walks over to talk about the prices of cotton,
candles, and tea, topics that seem to interest William
more than Caroline expected.

Gentlemen visit to discuss possible life on the moon
and admire the telescopes William is making.
Caroline sets scones and jam on the table.
Some gentlemen interrupt her. Others ignore her.
Her favorite visitor is Dr. Maskelyne
from the Royal Observatory, who keeps
close track of time as told by the stars and moon.
He and his wife let Caroline hold their baby as he talks
about women astronomers. *Hypatia, Elizabeth Hevelius,*
Maria Agnesi didn't seek fame or fortune, but worked
from devotion to their fathers, brothers, or husbands.

I work out of duty too. Caroline clears dishes.
There's so much in the sky. Is it so wrong to wish
for one small piece of her own? Or at least that William

would say, *Caroline, take a turn looking up.*
Sometimes she wishes he would raise his own teacup
to his mouth, butter his own toast.

The Mathematician

Most mornings Caroline makes coffee, stokes the fire,
stirs pudding. She brushes down the brown horse,
hitches on a bridle and saddle, and rides two miles
to the marketplace. Back home, she works on tables
and diagrams, adds to an old star atlas, interested
in what others overlooked. She measures star by star,
the way she knits stockings stitch by stitch;
maps the night sky, noting precise locations
of celestial objects, their size, brightness,
how they change, and the dates of discoveries.

She starts with one fact, lets math unlock more.
Her hand pivots as she follows the rotation of planets,
including Earth, whose movement creates the shadows
we call night and the brighter tilt of day. She teaches
herself calculus, which divides movement
into smaller and smaller steps, useful to fit
the sky's great circles onto paper.
Mathematics reaches like a wand that sweeps stars
to her desk, where she unfolds the light.

Escaping from Darkness
SLOUGH, ENGLAND, 1786

William leaves to deliver a telescope
to a German university, which gives Caroline,
now thirty-six, more time with the sky.
In the yard, she hitches her skirt and petticoats
above her ankles and climbs the ladder by the tall telescope.
Her foot falls asleep. Her neck aches.
No one can count all that shimmers above,
but mathematics suggests the enormity
and whispers when and where to look
for something never before seen.

Stars make her feel both lost and found.
One night she sees a nebula, a milky cloud
that's not on any charts. Another night
she spots brilliance that wasn't there yesterday.
A comet splits the darkness, giving a glimpse
of the faraway, brushing gold behind.

Caroline writes down the comet's location
and the time, calculates the differences between

the household clock and the celestial clock,
which reflects the four-minute switch in position
stars make each night.

Just before sunrise, birds chatter and chirp.
Caroline sings harmony as stars bow from sight.

Firsts

In the morning, Caroline addresses an envelope
to the secretary of the Royal Astronomical Society.
She dips the tip of a goose feather in ink:
As you are a friend of my brother's, I venture
to trouble you with the hope that my observation has merit.
She notes the location of the comet in relation
to three numbered stars, writes that her brother
is out of the country. She wants to make it clear
that she wasn't shirking sisterly duty
and also that she didn't need his help. She concludes:
I am, Sir, your most humble servant, Caroline Herschel.

The letter becomes the first paper by a woman
to be read at the Royal Astronomical Society.
The letter about what will be called the first lady's comet
is the core of the first report
by a woman published in a scientific journal.

Caroline riffles through the pages to see her name again.
She hums a tune no one has heard, imagining
a chorus thickening each note, and twirls.

Unseen

Another comet arcs through the black sky,
showering shine that disappears into darkness.
Caroline writes a note to Dr. Maskelyne
at the Royal Observatory, announcing her second comet.
Then she measures sugar to make gooseberry jam.

Not many days later, Caroline opens an envelope
edged with black and learns that her mother has died.
She cries because her mother never saw the sky
as she does: grand, friendly, wide as curiosity.
Because her mother never truly saw her daughter.

Alone

At fifty years old, William proposes to their landlady.
He tells Caroline, *Mary and I will keep two houses.*
I'll come here to use the telescopes, and you can stay.
I'll arrange to send you money each month.

Caroline doesn't want to be beholden
or go back to washing clothes or even making hats.
She's not a girl with her face half-covered with cloth,
more aware of what she's hiding than what she wants to see.
It's time I'm paid for my astronomical work, she says.
The king gives you a salary, William. I want one too.

The Beauty of Wages

King George III and Queen Charlotte are impressed
with the first lady's comet.
They hope Caroline might find more such tributes
to the empire and agree to pay her for her work.

Caroline becomes the first woman given
a salary for scientific research. Shouldn't bells ring,
trumpets blare, and dancers twirl in the street?
The world is quiet.

The Comet Hunter

Caroline moves her bed to a room over an old stable
by the house, spends almost every night on the flat roof.
Since she knows most of the intricate sky by heart,
she can swiftly notice unusual movement,
such as from a comet, which, coming from beyond,
gives clues about the depths of space.

Most nights Caroline sees nothing new.
Her long skirt billows in the wind. She sings to stay awake.
As she dips her pen in ink, her eyes adjust
from the dark sky to pale paper, because they must.
She won't ever have an assistant.

She spots another comet! Then goes to bed,
curls up her legs, rests the side of her face on her hands
until pale morning comes. She writes a report
she sends to Dr. Maskelyne at the Royal Observatory.

A few days later, she breaks the sealing wax on an envelope.
Dear Miss Caroline: Congratulations on the sighting,
though I implore should you spot another,

please hasten with such news. As you know,
comets are named after those who first spot them,
which in fact means an astronomer whose claim
first reaches an official. I fear this comet
was first reported in France.
Next time, do not use the penny post.

The Aunt

Night ends day, each with a new chance to behold
what's beyond. Stars keep Caroline company.
She discovers more comets, trailing
sprays of light, fading like memory at the edges.

Soon after she spots her fifth comet,
William and Mary welcome a son. Caroline loves
holding the small bundle of trust and curiosity.
She's even happier watching John learn to crawl,
later hearing short questions roll from his mouth.

When John is three, she defends him to his parents
when he draws geometric shapes on walls and climbs
the scaffolding around the tall telescope his father built.
Soon she sets up games and experiments
with teacups, canister tops, and pepper shakers.
The little boy she affectionately calls Sir John
often plays near her feet while she adds stars
and nebulae to outdated almanacs.
John stacks books into towers, looks through
some for pictures of constellations. He pretends

he's Capricorn the goat or Orion the hunter.
His favorite is Cancer the crab. Crooking his arms,
wiggling his spread fingers,
he exclaims, *We're going to the ocean!*

Yes. Soon. In August. Caroline wasn't invited
on this holiday. She kisses him. *You're beautiful and smart.*

I know. The little boy returns to star charts,
which interest him more than words.

Jam

What shines beyond what can be seen?
On the flat roof, Caroline, who was first,
or once second, to spot seven comets,
now sees a bright blur that may be another.
She needs another night to be certain,
but the following evening, rain falls
onto the thatched roof, bringing out the scent of straw.
Shortly after midnight, the rain stops. She looks again.

Caroline hums "Hallelujah," naps on the sofa
for an hour, then takes out her best parchment.
The post won't come for hours.
She winds a scarf around her hat,
saddles the horse, and shouts, *Run!*

The horse gallops or trots over dirt roads
until stars fade, the sky turns paler,
and birds wheel over meadows. They pass men
loading baskets of cabbages or tins of milk onto wagons.

She stops by a well so the horse can drink,
then at an orchard, where farmers pick plums.
One agrees to sell her a hatful of cherries,
since she doesn't have a basket or sack.
She eats them for breakfast, spitting out the pits.

By the time she reaches London, both she and the horse
are tired. But they've gone twenty miles
and can make it six more to Greenwich. She rides
over a curved bridge, looking down at washerwomen
wading in the river Thames. A grand clock tolls.

Then she's back on a dirt road that winds through a forest.
Finally reaching a moat, Caroline tugs the reins.
As the big gate is drawn, ducks swarm and scuttle.
Caroline slides off the horse,
hugs his damp neck, asks a stable boy
to fetch a bucket of water. She knocks on the door.
Her hands shake as she tells Dr. Maskelyne the news.

You are my worthy sister in astronomy,
he exclaims, then invites her to share tea
with his wife and their daughter, now nine years old.
Caroline wishes she'd saved some cherries.
Her legs are sore. She slips off her shoes
and puts a stockinged foot on the floppy-eared dog
dozing under the table. Could what women call "vain"
be what men call "pride"? She reaches
for another roll from a basket,
spreads it with a second spoonful of jam.

Her Book of Observations

When John is grown and studies the sky,
Caroline takes some time from her own research
to record his findings as she had for his father.
Later she encourages the young man in his choice
to study math in college,
then to marry a kind, curious woman
who's quite dazzled by his aunt. The family sails
to southernmost Africa to see stars hidden
beyond the horizon, which John observes and records.

Caroline adds these findings to her charts,
which show 560 new fixed stars, hundreds of double stars
where there had been merely a dozen on old maps.
She creates the first catalog of dark nebulae,
which suggest that stars and the universe change.
What shines is born, transforms, and flickers out.

Where have the comets she first spotted gone?
She doesn't need to know. Mystery is delicious.

Home

Caroline is hailed as the first woman to discover a comet,
the first woman to earn a salary for scientific research.
The Royal Astronomical Society praises her catalogs
of stars and nebulae and awards her a gold medal,
the first given to honor a woman's work.

Now seventy-eight, Caroline still signs her letters:
Humbly, yours. She's a sister, aunt, daughter,
assistant, and astronomer, who created
new ways to know the distances between stars.
A girl who was warned not to expect much
saw more of the universe than almost anyone before her.
Caroline Herschel makes the sky, vast as wonder, home.

MAKING CHANGE
WITH CHARTS, PART I

✦

FLORENCE
NIGHTINGALE

(1820–1910)

A Girl's Education

Florence offers drops of water to a bird with a bent wing.

Her mother doesn't complain about that, but she finds faults

in fractions of Florence, tells her not to tramp

through fields, bandage a farmer's limping dog,

or study mathematics books in the stable.

The maid who braids Florence's hair and buttons her dresses

in the back complains that burrs and brambles stick in the silk.

The governess wishes Florence

was more like her older sister,

who doesn't study spiders or champion families of mice.

She's not the first governess to go.

When Florence turns thirteen, Father takes over lessons

in history, languages, composition, physics, and astronomy.

He's not skilled in Florence's favorite subject, so orders

mathematics books and arranges for a cousin to tutor.

Florence likes balancing columns of numbers,

checking sums and being certain she's right.

Subtraction is soothing, though she dislikes

landing on zero. Something is missing. She wants more.

Divided

Mother says it's proper to bring beef broth,
jellies, and egg pudding to the sick in the village.
Florence should pray for the poor, but not give away
her own shawl or linger in a farmer's cottage
to wipe feverish foreheads. Mother believes
Florence takes goodness too far.

God loves all people alike, she reads in the Bible,
but the history of England insists on differences.
Florence tends to sick babies of families who live
in homes smaller than any of the fifteen bedrooms
in the Nightingale manor. She steps back out
into air scented with wild roses.
Chickens cluck as a rooster struts, flings back
his head so sunlight strikes the red coxcomb.

The Palace Garden

Queen Victoria, crowned last year, is nineteen,
and Florence eighteen,
when rich girls are presented at the court.
Mother orders her a white dress from Paris.
A maid elaborately twists and pins her smooth hair.

Florence bends her knees to the proper angle,
gathers her skirt to the correct height.
As she shuffles backward, careful not to turn the wrong side
to royalty, she wonders what the queen thinks about power:
she can rule an empire, but no woman can be a member
of Parliament, preach, go to a university, or vote.

Outside the throne room, duchesses raise china cups,
wave silk fans, then snap them shut.
Florence steps to the garden, where a field spider
scuttles in circles, raising a leg to make a web.
Each fragile strand shows her where to go next.

Seeking

During her twenties, Florence tutors factory girls,
translates German articles for her father,
dances at balls, inventories the household silver, and
makes fifty-six pots of gooseberry jam one afternoon.
She turns down proposals from two good men.
While she's not certain of what she wants to find,
she believes marriage might limit her views.

Florence sets down her embroidery hoop. Its stretched
fabric had multiple tiny squares, places to stitch
small crosses of varied colors that build a picture.
By candlelight, she reads books about hospitals,
learns that most offer surgery and medicine,
but no one to make sure
patients are eating, sleeping, kept clean and calm.
She tells her mother, *I want to be a nurse.*

That's no work for a lady. Mother approves of those
who might faint when faced with blood or naked skin.
She hopes Florence's restlessness will be cured
by traveling with a maid to chaperone and tend to her hair.

In Egypt, Florence sails down the Nile River,
rides a camel across the desert and climbs a pyramid.
In Alexandria, carrying two chameleons in her pocket,
she tours a hospital run by nuns.
In Greece, she rescues a baby owl fallen from a nest
from boys who poke it and laugh.
She strolls among stone relics and temples in Rome
with Lord and Lady Herbert and other British tourists,
eating hot chestnuts from a folded handkerchief.
She spends half an afternoon lying on the Sistine Chapel
floor, looking up at Michelangelo's painted ceiling.

What she sees is astonishing, but Florence wants more.
In Germany, she finds a new job for her maid
and books a room in a hospital run by a religious sisterhood.
At thirty years old, for the first time
Florence parts and pins up
her hair herself. After months of caring for patients,
she's awarded a nursing certificate by the nuns.

The Chance

Florence takes a job
at the Institution for the Care of Sick Gentlewomen,
where she's an excellent manager as well as nurse.
After England, France, and Turkey declare war
on Russia, her old friend Lord Herbert asks for help.

Florence buys and packs portable stoves, spare pairs
of sturdy shoes, a toolbox, and binoculars.
She buys white caps to keep her hair off her face
and dark dresses: none with hoops sewn in the hems
that would keep her from getting close
to those who need help.
She recruits thirty-eight more nurses, mostly
Protestant or Catholic nuns, to take a train to the shore
where ships bring soldiers shot on battlefields.
In November 1854, when she and the nurses arrive
at the hospital, a general says, *Go home.*
This is no place for ladies.

Florence doesn't turn back. She makes plans
and meets newspaper writers who are shunned

by military officers who dislike
their grim reports about deaths and battles lost.

Late one afternoon, Florence finds her binoculars,
watches birds swoop over the Black Sea. The sky darkens.
She sees Venus, Mars, and a bright spot
that might be Saturn, once thought to mark
the farthest part of the universe, but that changed.

Breaking Rank
TURKEY, 1854

At last doctors admit they're desperate for help.
On the Crimean Peninsula, for the first time
women nurse British military men.
The thirty-nine nurses get seven rooms for storage,
work, and sleeping. They're allowed two cups of water a day.
Florence chooses clean hands and face over tea.

She counts buckets, brooms, beds, twenty chamber pots,
and seven latrines for more than six hundred patients,
some lying on floors or in tents set up around the building.
She can't count the smell, blood, flies, fleas, rats, or screams.

Doctors tell her how military men are ranked and say,
We treat officers before the common soldiers.

Florence doesn't care about badges or buttons
embossed with swords, stars, and wreaths.
The world is not meant to be so divided
between rich and poor, generals and infantrymen.
She tells the nurses, *Care for whoever is sickest first.*

The Hammer

Florence seeks ways to get more clean water, healthy food,
blankets, a little peace and order. She measures
the inches between beds to document crowding,
takes notes on how many enter the hospital
and how many leave alive.
She's too busy to compare records from before
she came and now, but looks forward to doing the math
when she's not cracking open windows,
ordering two hundred scrub brushes, cleaning
for patients' comfort and to stop the spread of disease.

When she asks doctors to wash their hands
and surgical knives between treating patients,
they say, *Don't tell us how to do our job, Miss Nightingale.*
They refuse to unlock the closet where medicine is stored.

Florence doesn't have time to wait for them
to dole out what can heal. Patients need help now.
She finds a basket and hammer. She folds her hand
around the hammer's smooth handle and aims it at the lock.
The metal cracks. The cabinet door splinters.

She scoops up tinctures, salts, tins of pills,
extracts, and fills the wicker basket.

She carefully measures and records the doses
given to patients grateful for the gentle touch
of her uncurled fist. After dark,
she quietly carries an oil lamp, checking bandages
and fevers, listening to soldiers who can't sleep.
Some reach out to touch the shadow she leaves behind.

One Plus One

The nurses struggle to keep men still during amputations.
They help others stand and walk,
hold the hands of dying men.
Some nurses become ill themselves, or are homesick,
sad, scared, or stung by the doctors' insults.
Within weeks, a quarter of them go back to England.

Florence is exhausted but keeps on,
asking patients on the mend to care for other soldiers,
bidding their wives to wash clothes,
mop floors, and sew sacks to stuff with straw.
Needing more help, she talks to reporters
who are grateful she's given them stories
to write with both honesty and hope. Reporters organize
fundraisers for medicine, food, and warm clothes,
write that soldiers call her an angel
or "the Lady with the Lamp." They don't mention
doctors call her "the Lady with the Hammer."

Ledgers

As Florence tends to patients, she notes and tallies
who gets better and who worse. Counting helps
keep her calm, but she steels herself for subtraction.

Long past midnight, she addresses letters to England.
She sends families a soldier's last words
and sometimes the remains of his salary.

She asks some people for help, thanks
those who send socks, soap, flannel, doormats,
raspberry preserves, and ginger biscuits.
The queen, having heard that hospital smells
are unpleasant, offers to send a case of eau de cologne.
Florence gracefully declines. She wishes
everyone would save postage and just send money.

After the War

Florence returns to England ill herself, deeply tired.
She is the second-most-famous woman in Europe.
The most famous invites her to the palace.

Florence is highly praised for saving lives,
but it's not enough. More wars are bound to come.
Diseases won't go away. Before visiting the queen,
she pores over her lists of patients, what ailed them,
the treatments, and the length of each stay.
She draws columns of those who lived or died.
Within six months of her arrival, the death rate
dropped from 42 percent to 2 percent.
Can she show that if one hospital changed,
with some addition and multiplication,
a single story can fan into many?

The busy queen may grant her three minutes:
longer than a curtsy, but shorter than sipping a cup of tea.
How can Florence tell even a little of what she knows
about sickness and health? Numbers can hold
more than words in the same small space,
but she doubts the queen has patience for much paper.

Florence makes diagrams to show at a glance
what the hospital was like when she came
and the more hope-filled one she created.
Bars of different lengths are set in rows
since amounts seen side by side tell more
than when shown alone. Still she needs more.
Mulling, she walks in the park, smells rosebushes,
spots a spiderweb's delicate and orderly patterns.

She rushes back home and draws a circle
divided into twelve wedges that stand for each month
of the year to show changes over time.
She adds layers within the slices, some protruding
like rose petals, notched like a rooster's red coxcomb.
Dates and causes of illness overlap and can quickly be seen
on her rose diagram, coxcomb graph, and pie charts.

Circles on a Tea Table

Florence curtsies to the queen, who thanks her
for her kindness. After niceties, Florence hands her
the rose diagrams and coxcomb graphs she created.
They show dates and causes of illness side by side
or overlapping, so connections can be seen at a glance.
Florence explains that hospital survival rates rose
when bedding, floors, and doctors' hands were clean.

The queen lifts her silk fan. Florence worries
she's being dismissed, but instead servants carry
in a pot of tea, stacks of biscuits, and silver dishes of jam.
The queen asks to hear more, listens, unbuttons
her white gloves, and looks over charts that show
that for every man who died of wounds from weapons,
about seven died from disease caught in the hospitals.

Queen Victoria's eyes grow smaller, as if she's pinching
back tears. She says, *This must never happen again.*
Please send this information to the war office.

Past the Window Frame

Settled in London, Florence gathers still more numbers.
She hammers out eight hundred pages of words
and two hundred more of graphs and charts
she sends to military men and doctors, who read,
discuss, and soon treat patients more effectively.

Florence founds the Nightingale Training School for Nurses.
For the first time, women can train in a hospital
not run by a church. In the course of her life,
Florence pens fourteen thousand letters, many advising
Americans working near Civil War battlefields.
She writes a book about nursing that shows the science
behind patient care that women have long given:
plants and flowers freshen the air,
clean bedding keeps disease from spreading,
and kind words create a steadier pulse and heartbeat.

Florence knows people are sick or dying not only in war,
but women, children, and men are at risk
right here in the capital of England.
To convince members of Parliament of the need for change,

she asks workers to count how many people live
in one room and the number of windows in a home.
She charts the sources of water and heat,
pipes and plumbing, if any,
to show how health and housing are related.

The world should be less divided, more fair.
Florence oversees studies of child labor, poorhouses,
and deaths from childbirth, making records
she hopes will convince city and country leaders
of the need for reform.
She tries to keep her aim steady as noon light,
though statistics are shaped not just by numbers
but also chance, wishes, and despair.
Even sturdy records have shadows that shift.

More

In Florence's old age, a lifeboat, a racehorse,
and babies are named after her. Admirers write ballads,
piano pieces, and books in her honor.
A pledge named after her
is recited by devoted nurses around the world.
Merchants print her portrait on grocery bags.
She becomes the first woman elected
to the Royal Statistical Society.

Florence is almost ninety when she puts down
her pen on a desk covered with stacks of letters,
some with sealing wax stamped with a crown.
She switches on a new lamp that needn't be filled with oil,
pushes back the lace curtains, looks out
at protesters who wave signs reading: VOTES FOR WOMEN!
Florence remembers the girl she used to be,
and silently, happily, counts women who want more.

EXPLORING CURRENTS

✦

HERTHA MARKS AYRTON

(1854–1923)

The Watch Repairman's Daughter
PORTSMOUTH, ENGLAND, 1861

A girl balances on a branch, peers through green leaves.
Her brothers shoot marbles, shout, skylark on the street.
Phoebe Sarah Marks, who's called Sarah,
jumps down from the tree, dashes up to the two rooms
over a shop, home to the family of nine.
The youngest crawl or circle the desk
where their father works. His hands
hover quietly as prayer over the insides of a watch.

Look inside. Look closer. Papa explains
that the hands of the watch go around
when the force of an unwinding spring pushes gears,
levers, and a wheel set to turn once an hour.
He puts his hand over his heart
the way he does when he feels ill,
which is more and more often.

Mama touches his wrist, listens,
the way he holds a watch to his ear,
hoping to make it work again.

Forever

Late one afternoon, the room grows dark.
The oil in the lamp looks low.
Mama drapes a mirror with cloth, lights candles,
wails as she hands the rabbi the prayer shawl
Papa brought from Poland. She says, *He's gone*,
and opens her arms to the children.

Sarah looks at the desk covered with tiny hinges,
brass pins, ridged wheels, and a disc delicately painted
with digits. She wants to promise Mama she'll fix
everything, but she doesn't know how.

The Seamstress's Daughter

At seven, eight, then nine years old, Sarah
hurries home from school.
She minds her little brothers and sister
while Mama sews shirts and hems sheets to pay the rent.
She teaches Sarah to cut straight lines of cloth
and measure circles to make collars for people
who aren't rich, but have more money than they do.
They stitch every day, singing old Hebrew songs.
Still, there's never enough food on the table.
In winter, everyone's feet are cold.

Chance

*I've boasted to your aunt Marion about how quick
you are with numbers.* Mama unfolds a letter.
*She wants you to come live with them and go to the school
she runs in London. It's better than the school in town.*

I promised to help you! Sarah hugs her youngest sister,
who now can walk but never talks or claps
when Sarah sings nursery rhymes.
What about my brothers? Will they come too?

*Girls need better educations than boys, not worse,
for none of us knows what may happen. I wish
I learned more than sewing, which doesn't pay much.*
Mama pulls her close. Sarah hears her heartbeat,
remembers her father listening to what was hidden inside.

A Girl's Education

LONDON, ENGLAND, 1863

Uncle Alphonse teaches the students French.
Aunt Marion shows them how to solve mysteries
with multiplication. Sarah loves math for its loyalty.
Numbers may disappear, but new ones take their place.

She shares a bedroom with two small cousins.
She teaches them to play leapfrog and climb trees,
saying, *You can go higher,* standing ready
to catch them if they tumble. She sews jackets for their dolls
from scraps of cloth, stitching pockets smaller than stamps.

The girls kiss Sarah, roll like puppies near her feet.
Still, she misses her quiet sister and noisy brothers,
wishes for a friend her age. Other students swing
jump ropes, but won't let her skip under the arcs.
They wear dresses with elegant trim and tucks,
make fun of the holes in Sarah's stockings
and the way her hair spirals out of her braids.
Even a teacher complains she should be neater.

The Haircut

Back home for Passover, Sarah feels safe
as a single number at the end of a crowded equation.
Her shoes pinch, but she won't tell Mama,
who already worries
that the youngest child is not quite right.
Sarah's brothers get into mischief and more.
But when Mama finds her crying, Sarah confides
that classmates tease that her hair is too big.
She begs Mama to cut it. Mama combs her fingers tenderly
through her dark hair, but when Sarah insists,
opens her sewing scissors. A mistake.
The cropped hair bounds out more wildly than before.

The Gray Cat and the Green Chair

By the time Sarah is thirteen, Aunt Marion has taught
her all the math she knows. Sarah's older cousin, Numa,
now gives her problems. He loans her books
he studied for his entrance exam to Cambridge University.

A wick sputters into flame as Sarah lights an oil lamp.
She bends over a desk, prying open equations
the way her father took apart pocket watches,
trying to make what sticks move again. She loves
how algebra often begins with *If*, puffs with possibilities,
twists on *then*, slides to new certainty.
But sometimes she feels lost,
the way she did when Uncle Alphonse spoke
quickly and entirely in French. She takes
her paper, pencil, and books to a green armchair,
taps the cat with her bare feet, finds familiar signs
that help her fumble toward understanding.
Wrong answers point ways to right ones.

Another Chance

Girls at her aunt's school turn sixteen, pin back their hair,
and wear dresses that cover their ankles. Graduation
means most will pour tea at parties, listening to gentlemen
while keeping their faces half-hidden with silk fans.

Sarah works as a governess, then teaches math.
In the evenings, she sews to earn more money to send home,
sometimes bringing her needlework while she visits
new friends. Numa introduced her to Ottilie Blind,
whose house shines with paintings the family brought
from Germany. There she meets Barbara Bodichon,
an artist slightly older than Sarah's mother,
who wears bright flowing dresses like those worn
by goddesses in Renaissance paintings.

Madame Bodichon talks about her suffragist group.
Ten years ago we sent a petition to Parliament
but still haven't won women's right to vote.
We'll keep fighting, but education is important too.
We're starting the first women's college at Cambridge University.

My father said I might go. Sarah, you should too.
Ottilie turns to Madame Bodichon.
She's clever at mathematics.

You forget I'm poor, Sarah says.

We set aside money for scholarships, Madame Bodichon says.
We've found students who excel in literature and the arts,
but fewer in mathematics, which some men claim
as their domain. We must show them
that we can do just as well there, if not better.

A New Name

Sarah tutors her friend in mathematics
for the college entrance examination.
Ottilie writes poetry in the margins.
She asks, *Wasn't your cousin the first*
Jewish student at Cambridge? We'll be the first girls.

Numa was first to do math. Sarah takes a breath.
I'm proud of being Jewish and where I come from,
but can't care about ancient tales no one can prove.
I'll join my mother for meals on holy days,
but my faith rests in facts and a better future.

You're like a girl in a novel I read. Ottilie raises a book.
She created her own rules and religion,
based not on men's laws but those of the goddess of earth.
I'm going to call you Hertha.

I'm no goddess. But the name
makes her feel strong, so she keeps it.
No one will call her Sarah again.

Wondering
CAMBRIDGE, ENGLAND, 1876

Girton College is part of Cambridge University,
but somewhat separate and not quite equal.
Ottilie complains about how closely
the new students are watched. *Some fellows seem to hope*
we'll fail. It's mean, but it makes me work harder to show
them not only I but other young women can thrive.

One professor complains he can't teach math
while watching his language because a lady is in the room,
Hertha says. *Some say math can make women*
go crazy or blind from squinting at small figures.

Or that too much education can give women
lung disease or keep us from having babies,
Ottilie says. *But not all gentlemen are so foolish.*

Like that fellow you write the poems about?
Hertha has no time for romance. She makes hats
and embroiders drapes to sell
so she can send money to her mother.

She works on inventions, such as a paintbrush
fastened to a watch spring, then strapped on a wrist.
The wavy lines on paper left by the brush
can be counted to measure a pulse rate.

Hertha joins the choral society and starts a fire brigade,
after convincing the chief that girls aren't afraid of ladders.
She forms a math club, which meets in the library.
One member shows them a gold medal in a glass case
among historical plaques and portraits. *It was given
to my father's aunt, who discovered eight comets.*

Hertha looks at the date: 1828. *Has any other woman since
won a medal from the Royal Astronomical Society?*
As Constance Herschel shakes her head, Hertha says,
I forgot your father is an astronomer.

*My mother aspires too, but as I'm the youngest
of twelve, you can see she's been busy at home.*

Hertha looks past the glass case. *Could we be the last women
asked to choose between having a family and science?*

The Gift

Maybe Hertha spends too much time away from her books.
When college ends and examination scores come back
she's closer to the middle of the class than the top.
She gives Madame Bodichon a hat she designed and made.
I'm sorry I didn't do better, but thank you for your faith.

Madame Bodichon examines the hat's velvet trim,
made with a series of isosceles triangles
folded over rectangles.
This is quite a feat of engineering. And your blood pressure
device helps me keep track of my heartbeat.
You want to invent things. Curiosity
will help you more than high grades on tests.

The Teacher

Cambridge University insists that diplomas go only to men,
but with her Girton College mathematics certificate
in hand, Hertha finds a flat in London.
She sews her own dresses with straight, elegant lines,
breathes deeper and walks faster in skirts
that skim just above her ankles instead of floors.
Each morning she pins her hair above the back of her neck.
Strands puff and twist in a dark halo around her head.

She teaches in a high school, often writing
her own math problems, telling students, *Don't just stare
at the problem. Step in. Turn around. You can't know
if a dress fits until you try it on. And if it doesn't, try again.*

Nets

Hertha works on more inventions, including
a water-pressure gauge and a measuring tool
for builders and bricklayers. The weight of metals
in her hands shapes her understanding of hidden math.
She sews, sees friends, and attends Ottilie's wedding.
She helps her move into a new grand home,
where Ottilie promises Hertha
she'll never stop writing poetry.

And I'll keep inventing, Hertha says. To find more time,
she leaves the high school to tutor math.
Some girls are talented, some unambitious. Some quit.
Hertha confides to Madame Bodichon
that she's having a hard time finding students.
*You might be hired more if you wore your hair
in a net,* she advises.

Hertha loves the woman who made her studies possible,
but she won't risk a slide to hiding parts of herself:
first her hair, then perhaps her hands, or memories
of being poor. Each part has made her whole.

Electricity

FINSBURY TECHNICAL COLLEGE, LONDON, ENGLAND, 1884

A new school offers night classes
in the science behind trades
such as plumbing, metal welding, and carpentry.
Hertha enrolls in the electrical engineering course,
along with two other women and 118 men.
The school looks to the future, not the past.
Women weren't expected, but they're accepted.
Builders hasten to add a ladies' room.

Hertha likes Professor Will Ayrton's lectures
about powerful waves no one can see, but they flash
through lightning or snap as static in woolen stockings.

Electricity can create noise, light, heat,
or make something move, Professor Ayrton says.
Scientists are perfecting a small microphone that records
patterns of puffs of air made when someone talks.
They can be carried on an electric current through long wires,
The pressure of sound waves shifts a stylus up and down,
making an imprint of the waves' frequency and shape.

The students measure the tension of voltage
and electric currents that pass between metals
or meet resistance,
noting when energy appears or is lost as heat.
Electricity must complete a circuit, though its flow
can be interrupted with a switch, stopping sound or light.
Hertha charts changes in currents.
Math seems to set forces on paper,
still as sleeping birds just before they soar.

New Lights

After the class ends, the professor asks Hertha
to call him Will. He wants to know about her patents
and gives her a paper he wrote about modern geometry
to critique. As weeks pass,
they enjoy dinners with friends, including Ottilie
and her husband, whose children they admire in the nursery.

One evening they stroll past boys lifting sticks to light
the gas lamps. *Some streets in southern London
already have the new electric streetlights*, Will says.
*Scientists are testing carbon, bamboo, cotton threads,
platinum, and horsehair as filaments
to make a glow in the vacuum of a bulb.*

His hair is as dark as hers, though not as curly.
His high forehead is pale, his eyes gray and gentle.
Under the cream-colored glow,
Hertha and Will imagine a brighter night sky.

Wings

One Sunday, Will invites Hertha to his house.
In the parlor, she admires a painting of sheep.
My wife, may she rest in peace, chose that. Will talks
about her brief career as a doctor before her death.
They walk to the kitchen, where he praises his housekeeper,
says, *Women won't be so housebound once we figure out
how to use electricity to run machines
to clean floors and dishes, wash or sew clothes.*

*My mother would save much time with a machine
that makes a needle move quickly,* she says. *But even
sewing machines powered by hands and feet cost a lot.*

*Electricity must not be just for the rich. Mr. Edison
is looking for ways to make a good and inexpensive
lightbulb and bury wires underground
so the power can go anywhere. That would mean a lot of jobs.*

Many should go to women, she says.
Anyone nimble with needles can knit electrical wire.

They talk some more about the possibilities,
before Will asks, *Would you like to see where I work?*

He carries a lantern to the attic. A pine table
is covered with levers, coils, magnets, beakers, and scales.
Tacked to the slanted ceiling
are two prints of swans in flight.
As Will kisses her neck, she sees the wide wings spread.

When he asks, *Will you marry me?*
Hertha thinks of her mother, almost always
with a baby in her arms or near her feet,
children running in or out of the house.
Hertha has so much to do already. Can she risk
her life changing? Will gently touches
her rippling hair. She says, *Yes.*

Another Name

Promising love and equality, the bride and groom
say vows to each other in Ottilie's parlor.
She becomes Hertha Ayrton. Will calls her
"Beautiful Genius," then shortens the nickname to B.G.

She brings bookshelves and pots of geraniums
to the attic, where she invents and patents tools.
By looking closely, asking questions, and noticing
what's alike in what first seem to have little in common,
she often finds something new.

She gives lectures to women on electricity,
free singing classes to laundry girls, and visits
Madame Bodichon, who's ill and housebound.
Sometimes Hertha opens the door to a poor man
wearing a tattered coat and thin, battered boots.
She wraps bread and meat from the icebox in newspaper,
offers spare socks she buys for such moments
and keeps in a drawer. One day she shuts the door,
feels unfamiliar movement inside her,
wonders whether she'll have a girl or a boy.

Life

Hertha holds the baby over her heart, listening.
She kisses each finger, the back of her neck and her bottom,
like a silent prayer that one day this child will love
every bit of herself as much as her mother does.
The happy parents name the baby Barbara Bodichon Ayrton
and bring her to meet the woman who gave Hertha so much.
I wish she'd been born when women could vote,
but we did what we could. Madame Barbara Bodichon's
words wobble because she's suffered some strokes.

Hertha sings old Hebrew songs to the baby.
Later she listens as the small child tastes words
with consideration, then spits some, often scrambled,
from her soft mouth. Hertha coaxes her to crawl.
By the time Barbara masters balancing on tender feet,
the neighborhood's gas streetlamps
have been replaced by brighter electric lights.
Soon enough the little girl runs down pebbled paths
in the park, feeds the birds.
Hertha teaches her to climb trees.
Gleeful on a branch, Barbara cries, *Mumma, come!*

Hertha glances at stern governesses pushing carriages
or eyeing boys dressed like impeccable sailors.
Hertha joins her daughter, peering down through leaves.

Seasons

Crisp leaves fall. Soft snow drifts on branches,
then buds curl open to more unfurling green.

By the time electrical wires are run through the walls
of Hertha's home, her child is learning
to read and do sums, though Barbara prefers gymnastics.
These are happy years, but for Madame Bodichon's funeral,
where Hertha prays with full love and fractured faith.

Barbara becomes more of a mystery as she grows up
into an independent girl, precious as what's invisible:
electricity, gravity, whatever lies beyond darkness.

Flickering

The chatter of people gathered to watch
moving pictures for the first time seems electric.
Hertha, Will, and Barbara grow quiet as the lights dim.
A curtain is pulled to reveal flickering images
of a locomotive hurtling down a track.
Some spectators scream, duck,
then laugh as they remember
that what they see can disappear, like shadows.

Hertha swivels in her seat to look back at a box
that holds a ribbon of film shot through with light.
As it unwinds, pictures blink past heads to skim a white wall.
The reel of film clicks as it's grabbed at punctured edges,
then, in split seconds, rolls on. Even over the piano music,
Hertha hears the machine's clatter and a hiss from the light.

After everyone leaves the theater, Barbara fidgets
with a necklace Ottilie gave her for her thirteenth birthday,
says she wants to shop with Ottilie's daughter.
They dash past a few automobiles that chug and rattle
among the horses and carriages.

Hertha slips an arm through Will's with affection,
but also because he's ill, his eyes and feet undependable.
She says, *I loved the moving pictures,*
but it's a shame the light made such a racket.

Arc lights are good for streetlights, lighthouses,
and searchlights, but they're too noisy
and glaring to use indoors. Will looks from his boots
to Hertha. *We have a few at work you could study.*

Bright

Hertha steps around buckets of water and sand
at the laboratory, where wires are looped over hooks
on walls. She takes apart an arc light to examine
two rods made of carbon, a good conductor.
Each rod has a different charge so heat and light
shift between them, building into a spark that stretches
into a blue-white light that arcs through warming air.

Hertha ties on a cotton apron, slips on goggles.
She smells the metals she grinds, tastes the dust.
As she moves the tips of two carbon rods
closer or farther apart, she watches how the flame's
width and height change the heat and sound.
She writes equations to explore the ways voltage,
current, and the length of the leaping electricity interact.
Her experiments are long equations, too,
though instead of numbers or symbols,
variables can be heard, smelled, or touched.

The technical college professors and students
drop by to ask questions, discuss their own

projects, make suggestions, or lend a hand.

But Will stops coming around. He says, *I'll leave this in your good hands, B.G. When a man and woman work together, some fools claim the chap did the important parts.*

Sounds and Silence

Hertha discovers the arc light's hiss comes from air
filling a crater where carbon burned away.
She softens the sound by changing the shape and size
of the rods and the space between them.
Ottilie and her family come to celebrate
the vastly improved light Hertha designed. The evening
is happy, though Barbara leaves before the cake is cut.
Will looks exhausted: some nights he can't sleep,
while other evenings he struggles to stay awake.

Hertha is invited to become the first woman
to join the Institution of Electrical Engineers
and to present a paper on electric arc lights.
She's the only woman in a hall of 359 men.
Speakers greet the crowd, saying,
My lords, gentlemen, and lady.

Hertha's reports on electricity, which she's developing
into a book, are also praised by the Royal Society,
but a man is asked to read her paper to the members.
Women can't join this society or speak from the podium.

Together

Hertha publishes a thick book,
bristling with equations, about the arc light
before returning to the Royal Society hall.
She sits among scientists and listens
to a slight, bearded man. Monsieur Curie describes
the hidden energy of radioactivity, explains
how he and his wife worked to find what's inside atoms.
He repeats the word "we," but most listeners see the person
at the podium, not the woman banished to the audience.

After the applause, gentlemen crowd around the speaker.
Hertha introduces herself to Marie Curie, looking down
at fingertips scarred by the element she discovered.
They talk in French about radium and their daughters.
A stranger joins them. He congratulates Marie,
then glances at Hertha, says, *I notice*
all successful women scientists work with a man.

So do men scientists, Hertha says. *Few people work alone.*

Pliers

Hertha crawls out from under the sink when she hears
Barbara come into the kitchen. *I tightened a valve*
so the faucet won't drip. Hertha holds up a tool.
Isn't it beautiful how pliers open and shut
like hands, but can pinch and pull more?

No. Other mothers host tea parties.
They don't work with dynamos or keep socks
in a drawer to give to beggars. Mum, those men smell.

Some folks are down on their luck. It can happen to anyone.
Hertha puts back the pliers that can hold tight and bend.

Ripples in the Sand

Hertha makes chicken soup, sets a geranium
near Will's bed, cracks open a window for fresh air,
as Florence Nightingale advised in her book on nursing.
Hoping brisk, salty air may improve Will's health,
Hertha books a room at a quiet inn on the seashore.

In the cozy room, she shakes a clean sheet over the bed.
Energy ripples from her grip to the rising and falling waves
of linen. The sheet snaps and billows down.
While Will naps, she walks along damp, packed sand.
The sea mirrors the gray sky. She shields her cold face
with her hands against the strong wind
that whisks foam off the tops of waves.
She crouches to get a closer look
at lines curving through sand.
While waves vary in size, these ripple marks look even.
How were they made? Questions hover
like the crest of a wave before it crashes.
She listens not for an answer, but a way there.

Hidden

Hertha hurries back to the inn. She tells a maid
carrying in well water that she'll skip a bath,
but takes a bucket to pour into soap dishes
and pudding basins she finds in the pantry.
As water slips over her hands, she hears its splash.
Her senses shape, too subtly to measure,
her knowledge of invisible forces within.

She continues experiments back home in London.
She sets glass troughs of water on rollers,
sprinkling in black pepper to track how the waves
she creates move up and down more than ahead,
spin fast near the center, then slow down.
She measures their speed, height, and width
and the distance between the ripples they leave.
Repetition and boredom instruct.

Her equations take account of the forces
of wind and gravity. She pares
numbers and symbols to only what's needed:
no one puts spare parts in a watch

just because they gleam. What's essential is as hidden
as the spring that sets the dial of a watch in motion.

She learns sand ripples aren't made by waves
pounding the shore, but take shape under water
flowing back and forth. The force of the spin
can make an irregular sand ridge, then more ridges
form along the sides, as regular as rhyme.

Tea and Cake

Hertha's discoveries about wave motion are praised,
but she longs for a practical use, such as she found
with arc lights. For those discoveries in electricity,
Hertha is the first woman awarded
a Hughes Medal from the Royal Society,
which still won't let women become members.

Ottilie hosts a party, but Will is too sick to come.
Soon Barbara escapes with Ottilie's daughter,
both fashionably dressed. After Hertha talks
about their daughters' plans for college and Will's illness,
she asks, *Have you been writing any poems?*

Ottilie shakes her head. *What I read
is so much finer than what I write.*

But none of those poems are yours.
Hertha pours cold milk into hot tea.
The light and dark liquids spin
around each other before swirling into one.

Socks

When Will's illness worsens, Barbara comes home
from college. After a few days, Hertha says, *I appreciate
your help, but don't you need to get back to your classes?*

*Mum, how can you spend time in the laboratory
when Daddy is . . .* Barbara pauses. *Sick.*

Work gives me some peace.

I'm not like that. Barbara looks straight across
the parlor. *You'll be disappointed by my grades.*

Other things are more important.

Barbara stands, opens a drawer, looks at the socks
Hertha stashed to give to unshaven men who knock
at the back door wearing torn jackets and worn boots.
Barbara opens her mouth as if about to again advise
against giving to strangers, but just silently shuts the drawer.

Dusk

Late one afternoon the house grows dark.
The clock someone forgot to wind is silent.
Hertha drapes black cloth over the mirrors.

Weeks after Will's funeral, Hertha finds it hard
to get out of bed, brush her hair, buy groceries.
Barbara comes over to fold her father's clothes
to give away. A few months later
they pack more of Will's things.
Barbara says, *Mum, you need to get back to work.*

My studies on waves and sand ripples are of no use
to anyone. And I was sent some of your father's things
from the laboratory. Hertha points to a crate.
That's their way of saying that while a wife can work
at the college, there's no place for a widow.

You always worked here, too, Barbara says.

The lighting in the attic is poor. It's cold in winter.

Then let's bring everything down to the parlor.
You like to experiment more than host tea parties.

In the attic, mother and daughter
put coils, gears, carbon rods, magnets,
troughs, and beakers in boxes to bring downstairs.
Barbara picks up the bronze medal from the Royal Society.
I'm proud of you. Has another woman won this yet?
When Hertha shakes her head, Barbara says, *That's absurd.*
Mum, come to a rally with me. I want you to meet someone.

Votes for Women
LONDON, ENGLAND, 1910

The streets are almost as crowded as they were earlier
that year for Florence Nightingale's funeral.
Two women just a little older than Barbara
stand on a platform
decorated with purple, white, and green banners.
A woman shouts through a megaphone, *Deeds not words!*
Another speaks of starting work
in a cotton mill when she was ten.
Annie Kenny holds up a hand with a missing finger,
says, *Women care. Our votes will lessen the danger
in mills and factories. We'll vote
to improve the bad pay and long hours.*

After the speeches, Barbara introduces Hertha
to a poet she met at the university. Gerald Gould
and Barbara talk about how they interrupt
meetings in Parliament
and their work on a census boycott.
Barbara says, *Until women count, we won't be numbered.*

Hertha believes the census collects useful information.
By refusing to share a few facts of their lives,
women might be punishing science and themselves.

As Barbara and Gerald cheer for women
who wrestle out of the grip of policemen
or duck under their swinging sticks,
Hertha shouts, *Deeds not words!*

Two Women Walk by the Sea
HIGHCLIFFE, ENGLAND, 1912

Marie Curie is also a widow when Hertha invites
her and her daughters to a rented cottage by the coast.
They ride bicycles, walk by the water, and swim.
Hertha loves the turn of the waves, the force
between coming and going. She picks up a stone
stamped with coils, once a shellfish or snail.

Back in the cottage, Marie chops and melts chocolate
she brought from Paris, whisks in sugar,
slowly stirs in fresh cream. Sipping hot chocolate,
Hertha coaches the two girls on their English.
She makes up math problems that delight Irène.

After the girls go to bed,
Hertha talks about Barbara's wedding to Gerald,
and how they've been heckling members of Parliament,
demanding votes and breaking shop windows.
Barbara says women have been asking politely for the vote
for decades and nobody listened. So it's worth going to jail.

When I left Poland as a young woman, the prisons
were filled with good people fighting for freedom.

I'm proud of her, Hertha says. *So is her husband.*
A poet, but Gerald also writes for newspapers.
Maybe he'll run for Parliament and turn things around.
I've been writing letters to newspapers and politicians.
I have a petition to free the suffragists that I hoped you'd sign.

Of course. Marie nods, scraping up a last taste of chocolate
with a fingertip, its skin cracked. *But I believe I help most*
by keeping up my research, showing what women can do.

Through the open window,
Hertha hears waves hurtle onto sand.

Air
1915

As soldiers leave England to fight in the Great War,
suffragists are let out of prisons. Women are now needed
to work on farms, in factories, hospitals, and shops.
Hertha meets chemists who make medicines and explosives,
a Girton College graduate who taught high school math
and now designs airplanes.
Two of her former students run a military hospital.
Women who live on the coast and wove fishing nets
now weave metal nets to trap submarines.
Some women do calculations for weapons.
Others drive trucks.

Hertha reads a report on the pale green gas
wafting into trenches where soldiers hunker with rifles.
The newspaper ripples as she turns back a page.
Could the force of a wave's hidden spin turn
not just water but air, pushing out poisonous gas?

Hertha rummages through a drawer crammed
with clothespins, corks, stray lids, springs and gears

from old watches. She takes out a leather glove—
its mate lost—scraps of wire,
and a pack of playing cards with some missing.
She folds these to make models of air-flappers,
cards hinged together
with strips she cuts from the old glove,
and waves them like small flags on short sticks.
She sets brown paper on fire,
funnels smoke into boxes wrapped in damp cloth
so the smoke, like the poison gas, turns heavier than air.
She tries out small variously shaped flappers and fans,
shakes them so they gather smoke, then spin it back
where it came from, pushing in a fresh stream of air
over matchboxes she set up as trenches.

A fan shaped like a snow shovel that's wide
where it scoops works best. It's not impressive.
It looks like a big flyswatter, but she makes some
that will sweep out smoke without being
too big or clumsy for soldiers to carry.
Now she wants more made and brought to battlefields.

History

Hertha writes letters to politicians. She attends meetings,
demands to see a general to show him her invention.
If mustard gas can move into a trench full of soldiers,
it can move out. This fan can quickly sweep out poison,
and is collapsible so it can be easily carried.

A fan? We're fighting a war, not hosting a tea party.
The military budget goes to weapons.

The gas can ruin their lungs and minds.
Men are dying.

Some scientists are working on large machines
with filters and motors to clear out the gas.
Ma'am, your idea is too simple to work.

By "scientists" she knows he means men
who don't work in a parlor
equipped with soap dishes, battered pie plates, and kettles.
She says, *Simple fans can work as well and will be cheaper.*

The general waves a hand to dismiss her.
But Hertha doesn't leave. She thinks of the women
building parts for ships and planes in factories:
welding propellers, gluing fabric on airplane wings.
Some women are code breakers, radio operators,
electricians, and engineers
who make ways to intercept messages.
Marie and Irène Curie haul X-ray machines
to the front lines.
They tell doctors how to save lives by scanning for bullets
or broken bones before aiming surgical knives.

You must try my invention, Hertha insists.
She keeps talking to this man and more. At last,
one hundred thousand Ayrton fans are sent to battlefields.

Waves

The end of the war brings rejoicing,
though some women working in factories and farms
are distressed to lose their jobs.
About eight million British women
win the right to vote, granted as if in thanks
for helping the country through a disaster.
But women still have plenty of rights to fight for. Soon after
Barbara and Gerald start a group supporting equality
and world peace, Barbara gives birth to a son.
Hertha kisses the baby's toes, fingers, and nose,
whispers, *Michael Ayrton Gould, what is hidden in you?*
She listens to his heartbeat as she did with her own child,
never guessing her daughter
would run for a seat in Parliament.

Barbara gives campaign speeches, saying, *My mother*
is an excellent electrical engineer. She also taught me
it's important to give sandwiches and socks to the needy.
But no one should have to knock on doors or beg.
I want to change laws so that no one is cold or hungry.

After Barbara loses the election, Hertha says,
I don't know much about politics, but I know
it takes inventors many tries before they find success.

I'm glad some other women won seats, Barbara says.
Now men complain women's hats get in their way.
The new legislators must walk
half a mile to a ladies' room, but it's a start.

Two years later Hertha, who's been working
on a new kind of fan to help firefighters clear smoke
and advising bridge builders about underwater forces,
rents a house by the sea. She watches her grandson
while Barbara runs again for a seat in Parliament.

The shape of the shore has changed
since Hertha was last here.
She hikes up her skirt as the little boy runs
across the rippled sand into the sea. A wave knocks
him down. Michael shrieks and pushes himself back up.

The tops of waves move faster than the bottoms.
The unstable crest tumbles. Sand shifts underfoot.

Gulls ride on the winds. Pebbles roll over one another,
clatter and scrape back under waves.
Beauty is what can't be caught.
Children fly kites to understand the wind,
pick up rocks to tell the earth's time.
Hertha wades deeper, crouches, scoops up water,
which turns invisible in her hands.

MAPPING
WHAT'S HIDDEN

✦

MARIE THARP

(1920–2006)

The Land

As the green truck rattles over rutted roads,
Marie Tharp sways and bumps beside her father.
They hike through fields, where he digs up dirt
he labels. One patch of soil may predict how tall
a field of corn may grow. Papa also tests for signs
of oil or water. *Vast lakes lie under the hard ground,*
he says. *Rock and water keep changing place.*

He puts down his shovel, then sets up a tripod.
He measures angles between where they stand,
the horizon, and a point overhead called the zenith.
Much must be known to make a map,
which he does for the US Department of Agriculture.
Papa explains how math saves time.
Instead of spending days hiking from one place
to another, counting steps,
he takes measurements and multiplies.

I'm not the first to note cliffs or curves in rivers,
Papa says as he picks up and pockets an arrowhead.

People who lived here before anyone had paper
found ways to make good maps.

Marie tests which tree trunks best fit in her arms.
They form circles like the middle of a globe,
but instead of curving in at the top and bottom,
the branches and roots spread out.
Her rubber boots leave footprints in mud
as she searches for abandoned bird nests,
snake skins, fossils, and feathers.
Earth is like a book the wise can read.
Marie turns over a rock, sees a spider scuttle.

Blue

Back home, Mama shifts cloth
under the sewing machine's needle.
Papa arranges layered, gritty, or smooth rocks
that hint at what's below. He draws maps
at the kitchen table. Across from him,
Marie spills colored pencils and sketches trees.

Papa's name won't go in the corner
where artists sign paintings.
Instead, a small scale shows how to change
the map's inches to land's miles.
When he finishes a map, it's time to move,
which they do again and again. At ten, Marie packs
a zippered case of pencils, a soft pink eraser,
a worn wooden ruler, and a compass.
She's too old now for the connect-the-dot puzzles
she once loved, her toy telescope that made the distance
seem closer, but blurred it, too. The night before they leave,
Mama spins a lock of her daughter's red hair
into a snail shape she pins in place.
The curl never lasts long.

Crowded among boxes on the back seat of the Model T,
Marie bunches Papa's blue flannel coat into a pillow,
remembers leaving Michigan; New York; Washington, DC;
and Alabama, where she stepped in the ocean.
They never stayed anywhere long enough
to make many friends, but she has all she needs.
She leans on a carton of *National Geographic* magazines.
Their spines shine like wet sunflower petals.
Some bloom with maps. She unfolds one
almost as wide as her arms can reach.

Days
BELLEFONTAINE, OHIO, 1935

Marie is fifteen when her family settles on a farm.
Papa's pockets still sag with a tape measure,
a jackknife, and a small worn notebook,
but as he plants carrots, onions, and corn,
he tosses rocks from the fields as if he's forgotten
each has a story about the age and history of Earth.

Marie claims a wooden desk that was left behind.
She drapes a tissue paper pattern over cloth,
studies geometry as she turns straight lines to circles
for a skirt. Her mother showed her how to line up
stripes, match plaids so the seams are almost hidden.
Now Mama spends much time in bed,
medicine bottles circling the lamp,
filling out requests for college catalogs
from all over the country, printing Marie's name.
As if she can bear to think ahead.

The Green Chair

Marie lines up numbers on sand-colored sheets
called math paper, almost as thin as tissues.
Small numbers stand for big ideas, the way
her father's earth samples spoke of fields and forests.
Math is as certain as stone, as efficient as language.
One can say the word "sky" faster than one can see it all.

She starts calculus, which can shadow
changes in celestial bodies, electricity, or growing plants.
Sometimes she murmurs over homework, *I can't do this*.
She never heard a boy say that, though enough
are baffled. Maybe boys find it easier to keep on
since they look more like the teacher, whose jokes
seem meant to make them laugh, not blink or squirm.

Marie fidgets on an armchair by an old china lamp
that casts pale yellow light. She writes possible answers,
groans, then backs up, hunting for the wrong turns.
At last what seemed like a curtain turns out to be a mirror.
She was here and capable all along.

Seasons

As the weather turns warmer, the chickens cluck
more loudly, lay more eggs. Marie draws pear blossoms.
Inside the house, the whir of the sewing machine
and snap of scissors turn silent.
Papa says the word "cancer" just once.
The smell of hamburgers and onions Marie fried lingers,
as she gathers homework in her arms.

Before the apples turn red on the branches,
Marie hears Papa cry behind a door.
The earth makes room for her mother.
Marie goes to the barn and shouts her name.
The sound echoes in the hayloft.

She stashes away her colored pencils and college catalogs.
New wheat blows in the wind.
She picks and snaps open beans, cooks for her father.
In the chicken coop, she gathers eggs as warm as her hands.

After petals dry and fall again from fruit trees,
Papa says, *Your mother wanted to settle*

on the farm, but you always liked to travel.

The man who never went to college says,

Nothing must stop you from learning.

Unforgotten

At the university in Ohio, Marie declares her major
first as art, then switches to English, music, math,
and finally geology, which her father taught her to love.
She's one of three women among seventy men.
Geology reveals how land and sea
shifted slowly and long ago.
The earth's crust might have broken under the forces
of underground waves that made gaps in the land,
tossed boulders that piled into mountains.
Could hidden currents have moved continents?
Most scientists say no. Such massive land couldn't drift.

As Marie picks up a fossil, she marvels at how a spider
or snail may be forgotten, but millions
of years later, traces and tracks remain in rocks.
She splits open granite and quartz,
but uses math more than hammers and picks.
She studies volcanoes and earthquakes,
which move in waves. The earth never stops changing.
She loves its hidden stories, but she doesn't believe
she'll find a job looking for those.

Instead, practical people
want underground fuel to run cars and warm homes.

She's hired by an oil company to keep accounts,
figuring out answers fixed in place. She's bored.
At night, she takes advanced math classes to earn
another degree and remember the pleasure of working
on proofs, which show that what's true once is true always.

Shore

Marie unfolds a map, heads east toward blue borders.
Sunlight spills into the sea, which shuffles and spins
its energy along in waves that slow and bend on shore.
Some children pick up rocks or seashells.
A girl grips the string of a kite.
Marie feels the sand and pebbles underfoot being tugged
back to the sea. She slips off her shoes, wades in,
surprised by the slant down. How steep is the slope?
Maps of the world no longer feature pictures of mermaids,
sea dragons, castles, or cottages for elves,
but much stays mysterious. Marie supposes the seafloor
isn't as flat as its surface, but does anyone know?

She wipes salt spray off her glasses, hooks a strand
of her hair behind her ears, remembers her father
swinging a shovel, wanting to know what was underneath.

Shine

Marie finds the Columbia University geology department
in a basement crowded with broken or battered furniture.
Metal tables are covered
with split rocks, microscopes, and ashtrays.
Dr. Maurice Ewing nods when Marie speaks
of her classes in geology and math. Her gaze shifts
from him to a table covered with photographs
of coral, starfish, crabs, moss, snails, squid, and ripples
left by currents. Trails and prints from sea creatures
look blurred as if seen through her old toy telescope.
And amazing. *You have pictures from under the sea!*

Some of the other fellows and I designed the camera,
Dr. Ewing says. *We drop it down from the deck,*
setting a flash for light where it never shone before.

How deep was this?

Some of the sea is two or three miles deep.

After she asks more questions, he puts down the papers

about her background. *You know a lot,*
but I'm more interested in your curiosity.
Everyone calls me Doc. When can you start work?

One

People drift between desks. No one tells Marie
where she should sit or what she should do,
but men ask, *Could you type this up, Miss Tharp?*
When she reminds them she's not a secretary,
some say, *Just do me this one favor. We work as a team here.*

She catches her breath, annoyed that the team
seems to have just one typist. But she says yes
when Bruce Heezen, who's taken research trips
on navy ships with Doc and cowritten many papers,
asks her to make graphs comparing the temperature
and saltiness of water, check the calculations
for underwater gravity and wave speeds.
Her math briefly shrinks the world, and then,
after pages of work, widens the view.

Marie designs charts for the men's presentations.
She improves maps by dropping one over another
on a table with a glass top. A light shining beneath
lets her see through the layers
and put the information together.

She likes the work but wants to follow a theory,
any not-so-wild guess, from beginning to end.

She straightens her glasses, pushes her hair behind her ears,
presumes she's treated differently because she's a woman.
She tells Doc, *I want a project of my own.*

He nods. *A house was just donated to the university for us
to use as a research center. How are you at packing?*

Waves

Steel file cabinets, boxes of papers, and equipment
soon fill a big house across the Hudson River.
Marie gets her own drafting table in an old bedroom
that she shares with two men.
The only phone is hung by that door.
In the former living room, she tacks up maps,
tenderly smoothing out wrinkles.
What's all that blue? A place not yet known.

In the basement of the Lamont Geological Observatory,
she and Bruce set up a seismograph,
which measures the strength of waves always moving
under land or sea. He says, *A lot of the work Doc and I did*
at sea was looking for places where earthquakes broke
the ocean floor and rubble piled into mountains.

She hears the electric pen scratch across rolling paper,
recording seismic waves: forces under the earth
or the sea's surface started by earthquakes or volcanoes
no one expects here in New Jersey. She wants
to understand the ways the earth is always speaking,
hinting at how its shape may change.

Division

Everyone at work cheers when the observatory wins
a big contract from the phone company.
Before new cable lines are laid undersea, one man works
at the desk by Marie's, studying temperatures
at the ocean floor, which could affect the transmissions.

The phone company wants to know
why old telegraph lines snapped where they did.
One theory is that underwater earthquakes broke them.
Howard Foster, the third person in Marie's office,
starts to chart the thousands of places
where earthquakes began in the North and South Atlantic.
He turns locations of earthquake epicenters
into a lengthening row of dots on a map.

It's a rote sort of work that doesn't ask for wonder,
the kind of task Marie is grateful not to be assigned.
But she's asked to help with it and other men's work,
not put in charge of her own. She looks at the rolled maps
leaning against a bare wall. She's not the only person
here who can handle thumbtacks or tape.
Let somebody else hang these.

If

Back from a research ship, Bruce and Doc spread
photographs that look speckled with salt. Marie catches
her breath at the glimpse of urchins, octopuses, sea spiders,
snails, and other creatures that scuttle or swim
near the ocean floor. As the men talk about undersea life,
Marie interrupts. *I want to go out on a research ship.*

It's not all great, especially when it rains.
Bruce is a large man who wears gaudy shirts
and black-framed glasses. *The food is terrible.*

*Don't tell me you believe that old superstition
that women at sea bring bad luck.* Her hope snaps.

Don't take it personally, Bruce says. *A fellow wants
to burp and fart or talk without worrying
we'll offend a lady. We all share one toilet.*

Women aren't allowed onboard navy ships,
Doc interrupts. *We can't change the country's rules.*

Marie gazes out the window past trees to the river.
For four years she's filed other people's papers,
checked the facts on their reports,
copied maps instead of drawing her own.
Each time she organizes information she didn't collect
feels like weight put on her shoulders.
She tells Doc, *If I don't get a project of my own, I'll leave.*

The Question

Bruce and Doc lug cartons into the old bedroom.
Doc nods at Howard, who is deaf, and the other man,
who keeps working. Marie reaches into one carton,
unrolls sheets of long paper marked with records
of the sea's depth at particular places. These soundings
are made when an electric ping is shot down from a ship,
while a machine onboard records how long it took
for the sound to bounce off the bottom and back.

We've been collecting soundings for five years,
covering thousands of feet of the ocean floor.
Bruce pushes up his thick glasses.
He smells a bit like a beach.
We don't know what to do with them. What do you think?

I don't know. Her answer sounds like an end
but can be a beginning. Finding
out more could take a long, thoughtful time.

Searching

Before Marie can look for secrets in the soundings,
she must put them in order. She starts with some
from the Reykjanes Ridge off Iceland,
then moves south, calculating longitude and latitude
to mark where the soundings were taken.
She matches wavy and straight lines
showing depths, the way she once fit together
stripes on cloth for the seam of a skirt.

She makes crosses to mark the sources of soundings.
Some were taken recently from ships with sonar
and some are old, collected by sailors
who dropped weights tied to knotted ropes,
then pulled them back up and counted the knots.

Her map is the same scale as Howard's map,
with one inch standing for about eighty miles.
Some of her work will help determine the size
of the undersea phone cables:
long enough to pull over peaks, but not wasted on plains.
She might find secrets no one has thought
to look for in depths no one has seen.

Discovery

A picture of mountains in the middle of the Atlantic
slowly takes shape under Marie's pencil.
The range is longer than that of the Appalachian
or Rocky Mountains. She measures peaks
higher than the tallest mountains on land.
Sketching to show the varied heights, she notes
a pattern as subtle as a brown feather woven into a nest.
Others knew there was a mountain range, but not
the long cavern cutting through the middle of the peaks.
The cut in what she'll call the Mid-Atlantic Ridge
is about as wide and deep as the Grand Canyon.

She hears the click of the machine wired to the one
in the basement tracking signs of earthquakes.
The land seems so still, but all along what's hidden
hints at how quickly the earth can change.

Volatile

Marie works with more measurements,
stumbling past blocks and around detours
to a single certain answer. She depends on math
as she draws a map, letting curved and crisscrossing
lines stand for the cavern. She points out the gap
in the mountains to Bruce, who says, *I don't see it.*

Look harder. Recognizing a pattern is like spotting
the truth in a trick. She says, *No other range of peaks
has a gully on top. That gap could show where North
and South America split from Europe and Africa.*

Continental drift? Scientists ditched that idea long ago.
He shakes his head. *There's no proof.*

This could be evidence. She runs her palm over her work.
She knows most scientists agree with him
and change ideas slowly.
But it seems the earth is alive,
its crust like sheets of ice that crash together,
making mountains and leaving gaps.

Talk like that could wreck your reputation,
Bruce says. *You'd better measure everything again.*

Proofs

Marie spends more months checking numbers
that stand for the depth of water, weather, the time of day,
and the speed of the ship when the soundings were taken.
Some equations sprawl. Others stick,
so she circles back to the beginning,
which holds what she needs to know.
Signs of a cavern
about twenty miles wide and a mile deep remain.

Science leans on facts, but new ideas begin in spaces between,
with guesses bouncing between right and wrong.
Did land pull apart leaving a crevice or break,
spewing rubble that formed mountains?
She shows Bruce her maps and figures.
I think this is where continents broke apart.

Marie, no one will take you seriously if you talk like that.
Bruce crumples a wad of paper, then throws it at the wall.

Don't shout. It's bad for your heart.
She glances at the pocket of his floral-print shirt,
where he keeps a pillbox.

Even if the theory of continental drift is sound,
no one wants to hear it, he says. *Nobody wants*
to think of land as something that can break apart.

That happened millions of years ago, Marie says.
People shouldn't worry their houses will drop into the sea.

Excursions

Marie and Bruce argue about the canyon and its causes
over dinner and on weekends, driving up
rough back roads, stopping at antique or junk shops,
where she looks for wooden ducks for her collection.

Both have separate projects now but work together, too.
One day they paint over the pale colors on globes
with dark blues, brown, and black to add new findings.
She rubs off spatters of paint on the side of his neck,
lets her hand rest a moment under his ear.
Five minutes later, they bicker about the shade of blue.

Parallel

As Marie talks on the phone, pulling the coiled cord
from the wall, her eyes rest on Howard's map.
A band of spots mark the sites
of earthquakes where cables broke.
Connecting the dots, she sees a familiar shape.

Hanging up the phone, she waves her hands
to ask if she can drape his map over hers,
which she lays on the light table. As the beam
penetrates the overlapping papers,
the places where earthquakes began
line up with the Mid-Atlantic Ridge.

Marie's hands turn cold. She shouts with joy.
As Doc and Bruce run into the room, she says, *The force
of all those earthquakes could have split continents.*

Maybe, Bruce replies.

We'll look into this more, Doc says. *And meanwhile
keep it quiet so no one thinks we're crazy amateurs.*

Matching Shores

In the Lamont Observatory kitchen, Doc talks
about scientists who discovered that the types and ages
of some rock on opposite shores of the Atlantic are similar.
A certain kind of snail is found only on the northern coast
of North America and Northern Europe.
That snail can't swim across the sea.
A rare species of spider
was found on lands now an ocean apart.

Mathematics also shows how continents
almost surely shifted.
Euler's theorem is used to calculate
the rotation of continents' edges
and show how the lands once fit together.
At last Bruce and Doc agree to make these findings public.

When Marie picks up their report on continental drift,
her face gets hot. *Why isn't my name here?*

It's the information that's important, Doc says.
Bruce and I have collaborated on other reports.

Our names are better known,
so this will get more attention.

I'm not looking for fame, but fair is fair.
As Marie feels her voice shake, she raises it.
This is my work too. Don't forget that.

The Floors of the Ocean
1959

Marie draws up many charts. Her ideas are added
to those of Doc and Bruce for the first book
that scientifically describes the bottom of the sea.
All their names go on the cover.

Water

Bruce offers to care for Marie's dog when she returns
to the farm where the earth makes room for her father.
In the old house, she packs his arrowhead collection,
his favorite blue coat, and her mother's sewing machine.
It must have rained sometimes, but all she remembers
are blue skies over the fields where she and Papa walked.

When she gets back home, she winds thread
around the bobbin the way her mother twirled
her hair before pinning down the spiral.
She patches her father's coat with yellow and red threads.

Adding money he left in his will to her savings,
Marie buys a house near work and Bruce's home.
She fills it with a leopard-skin-print sofa,
a carpet patterned with green waves, her collections
of carved ducks, beautiful masks, rocks, and globes.
She's close enough to the Hudson River
to hear small waves lap the riverbank in summer,
see ice glisten in winter.

Finding a Way

Every map is a compromise.
Road maps might leave out creeks.
Most city maps don't show houses.
Maps depend on the lean art of subtraction
and geometry, starting with one point and a line.
A round earth on flat paper demands distortion,
so Marie uses spherical trigonometry to
account for the curve of the earth.

Drawing, she begins at the edges of continents,
the way that when working on puzzles
she starts at the borders.
The symmetry of the Atlantic makes her hum.
Her grip on her pencil is attentive and tender.
She shifts the pencil tip with the earth's rise and fall,
makes thick lines to show steep slopes
and slender lines for underwater plains.
Her thick-thatched lines show where masses of land split,
their edges piling against each other in mountains
that fill most of the center third of the Atlantic.

The intricate, accurate drawings take a long time.
Figuring out what to draw takes still longer.
She fills in some spaces first left dark or dappled,
treating the data with respect, but guessing
about shapes between known parts of all oceans,
which cover almost three-quarters of the world.

Marie marks where the Atlantic ends
and the Indian Ocean begins, though she dislikes
suggesting borders when clearly it's all one ocean.
The map won't be truly finished until
the entire seafloor is known, which may be never.
Every map marks places
where another journey might begin.

First

Numbers and symbols wash across Marie's wide desk.
Finding order within equations that warp
into new problems, she gets weary.
But beauty lies hidden under her hands.
So others might see what's bold as the sea itself,
she works another hour, another day, another year.

Marie maps a range of mountains beginning near Iceland,
running through the Atlantic. As more information
is brought in over a decade, she sees
that the mountain range continues around Africa,
across the Indian Ocean,
and through the Antarctic and Pacific Oceans.
All along, connections were waiting
to be noticed by the astoundingly patient.
What they called the Mid-Atlantic Ridge
is part of the Mid-Oceanic Ridge.
No one before has connected these mountains,
which run for about forty thousand miles around the world.
No one has accurately drawn
this much of what's under the sea.

Sunday Morning
NYACK, NEW YORK, 1972

Standing in the kitchen pouring coffee,
Marie wears a white shirt and a skirt she made
by cutting her father's blue coat into strips
that are wide at one end and more narrow
where she sewed the waistband.
She and Bruce quarrel over some questions
from the publishers at the National Geographic Society.
Bruce talks about going out on a submarine.

Marie feels a pang of jealousy. She gives a treat to her dog,
then unfolds a newspaper and reads about a new law,
Title IX. It means that girls who can throw a baseball as well
as boys can't be kept off teams in public schools.
And it seems that women who can do science
and work with a crew shouldn't be kept off ships
that belong to the country.
Marie puts down the newspaper and picks up the phone.

Partings

ICELAND, NEAR REYKJANES RIDGE, 1977

Waves sweep in, turning blue to green and white.
Bruce will be one of twelve men on a submarine,
sleeping in shifts on four bunk beds and sharing one toilet.
Marie touches the side of his face, his rumpled shirt,
printed with palm trees. The left pocket swells
with mechanical pencils and his heart medication.
If she were his wife, and she's mostly glad she's not,
she'd have to remind him to take those pills,
ask if he packed everything.

Our map should be back from the printers when we return.
We'll have champagne and cake.
Bruce wraps his large hand around hers.
We couldn't have found a bigger or better job.

Not on this planet. Marie looks up at the wide sky.
She kisses Bruce, will miss him. But norms and laws
have changed. This time she won't stay on shore.

The Darkness under the Sea

Small waves hit the hull of the research ship.
On the deck of the *Discovery*, Marie makes her way
around big spools of wire, cables, toolboxes,
and crates of spare parts.
She catches her balance as the ship skims
over the world's longest mountain range.
She and other scientists drop a cage of instruments
to check the water temperature, the strength of the salt,
measure currents and magnetic forces.

Marie is watching a whale break the sea's surface
when a message comes over the ship's radio.
She learns that Bruce's heart stopped
while he was deep underwater. *No!*
Was he lying on the floor before a porthole, marveling
at the seafloor and what lives just above it?

On the *Discovery*, coworkers approach Marie,
their arms rising and lowering,
like seagulls not sure where to land.
All the scientists here knew Bruce.

The sounding machine clicks and pings.
Rustling paper unwinds with new soundings
recorded by a spark that burns dots on paper.

The ship filled with mourners turns around.
The deck rocks as the ship pushes through its own wake.
Then the sea returns to wrinkles.
Below, the sea's vast darkness
is like a night that never ends.

Back Home

Marie tucks her head against her dog's soft black ears.
Then she walks over to Bruce's house,
rummages through his closet, fills her arms
with bright shirts and two pairs of trousers.
She plugs in her mother's sewing machine,
patches together a skirt the way she did
when her father's coat became torn beyond repair.

The World Ocean Floor Panorama arrives in the mail.
The names *Marie Tharp* and *Bruce Heezen*
are printed in the corner.

Hey, Bruce, Marie calls softly. There's no echo.
But she imagines his grin as magazines
as bright as sunflowers are opened in offices.
In a living room, a girl unfolds the map,
holds it between outstretched arms.

CREATING PATHS THROUGH SPACE

✦

KATHERINE JOHNSON

(1918–2020)

Prophecy

Katherine counts eggs she gathers in the chicken coop.
She counts peaches gently placed in a basket,
counts not just spoons but the beat of their clatter.
She crouches to listen to a cricket.
She loves best what she can't count:
raindrops, leaves rustling into a chorus,
stars blinking in and out of sight over the hills.

In church, Katherine counts girls with braids,
women wearing hats, and men with shut eyes
who may be dozing. At school, her hand splits
the air as she asks what no one else wonders.
She's sent straight from second grade to fifth.
Her teacher's look lasts long, as if she sees
not just the girl but who she might become.

Beyond

Katherine's father works on their farm, does carpentry
for some white families, sweeps the floor of the library,
where his children aren't allowed to check out books.
As they walk home, Katherine takes two steps
for each one of his. He can look at a patch of pine
and guess how many trees fill a forest.
A single branch of pink blossoms tells him
how many apples may ripen on the whole tree.

I went to a school that stopped in sixth grade,
he says. *White folks still claim the high school
is just for them, but I learned of two schools
in West Virginia where you'll be welcomed.
Katherine, the world is bigger than this town.*

The Curving Road

Crowded in the back with her sister and brothers,
Katherine hears the engine's sputter and grind
as their father turns the key to a friend's truck. *Let's go!*
We've got a right to drive down any road,
but if we need to stop, it can't be just anywhere.

Daddy sings, keeping his eyes straight ahead.
Katherine looks at the road as if memorizing an equation.
Her father often tells them:
You are as good as anybody around, but no better.

The words move through her like a hymn.

Neighbors
INSTITUTE, WEST VIRGINIA

The family rents a house near the Kanawha River
and a library. At last Katherine can check out a book
from shelves as straight as the lines calling for division,
with dots above and below that say: Go!
She borrows more books from neighbors whose parents
teach in the town's all-Black school or the college beside it.

New friends invite Katherine to play double dutch.
They turn their wrists slightly so two clotheslines
twirl in wide circles. *All in together, girls.*
How do you like the weather, girls?
Katherine skips over ropes, almost safe within semicircles.

A Girl's Education

Katherine folds her hands on a wooden desk.
She likes math, full of equal signs and question marks,
English, French, every class but history,
which seems bent on making girls like her invisible
or in need of rescue. She'd rather look ahead than back.

Katherine loves the swoop of her math teacher's arm
before the board black as the night sky.
Miss Turner introduces the sign for infinity,
like the numeral eight lying on its side.
Katherine is fourteen when her teacher asks her
to join her for supper, talks about going north
in the summer to earn an advanced degree
in math at Cornell University.
On the porch, sitting on green wicker chairs,
Miss Turner names the constellations.
They both love what can't be counted or divided.

Probability

Katherine's family spends summers back
in White Sulphur Springs. Daddy works at a grand hotel,
carrying luggage for white travelers.
He's thankful for each and every job, especially
during the Depression, when many have no work,
and saves so all his children can go to college.

Katherine pours crystal pitchers of lemonade,
polishes a table in the lobby, as her father greets
returning guests. He says, *Welcome back, Mrs. Lodge.*
Good afternoon, Mr. Taylor. Her father's nod is deep.
As he picks up suitcases,
Mr. Taylor says, *Thank you, Joshua.*

Katherine holds both ends of her dustcloth over the table.
It droops in the middle, like a broken equation.
Her father addresses white people with respect,
but they call him by his first name, as if he's a boy.
They can't see the gentle man
who's kind to all, an untrained mathematician
who can look over a golf course

and calculate, from the arc of an arm,
how high a ball will soar and where it will land.

Another guest asks for the bellman.
The manager snaps his fingers, calls to her father,
Uncle Joshua, you're needed here.

Katherine shakes out her dustcloth, considers weights,
variables, and probability: What would happen if
those who used a first name heard theirs in return?
What's polite enough speech for one person
shouldn't twist to defiance in another,
but bend like a Möbius strip with only one side.

But they're in a hotel where she, her father, or others
with brown skin may not dine at the tables they set,
sleep in the beds they make up,
or play croquet on the wide lawns they mow.
Katherine looks at her father, who raises his eyebrows,
which means: *Don't say anything.* Then lifts
one corner of his mouth, as if to add, *Not yet.*

The Chalkboard

At fifteen, Katherine starts college. Her favorite class
is with elegantly dressed Professor Claytor,
who doesn't bother with greetings
as he strides into the classroom,
plucks chalk from his pocket, turns to the blackboard,
and continues an equation where he left off the day before.
He writes with one hand, erasing
numbers with the other to make room for more.

Katherine finishes all the college math classes in two years.
Professor Claytor creates courses just for her,
lecturing loudly and clearly as if every seat
in the classroom was full. He introduces Euler's formula,
which includes an astonishing *e* that grapples with infinity.
Katherine no longer looks for right answers
but learns to keep afloat in a sea of questions.
She learns to refine the skill of guessing,
making estimates that might lead
to what no one knew before.

Just before she graduates, Dr. Claytor says,
You could go on to do research, maybe teach in a college.

He is the third African American
to earn a PhD in mathematics,
writing a thesis on the geometry of space
at the University of Pennsylvania.
But while he could take graduate classes
in the North, no college there would hire him to teach.
She asks, *Where could I find a job?*

That will be your problem, Miss Coleman. Mine
is to make sure you're more than ready for whatever comes next.

She looks past him to the blackboard. The chalk
was erased, but traces suggest ways through the unseen.

The Teacher
MARION, VIRGINIA

Katherine finds a job teaching math and French
in a school that's segregated, like all those she attended.
After classes, she plays piano and instructs the chorus,
corrects papers in her classroom rather than walking
back to the room she rents at the principal's house.
Sometimes she watches the chemistry teacher
coach football, basketball, or baseball.
After a game, they walk together.
Jimmie laughs as he describes a student struggling
with a test who got up from his seat to sharpen a pencil.
He spun the handle like a fishing reel,
pretended to hold on to a rod and pull in a fish.

Katherine thinks she would have sent the boy
straight back to his chair, but Jimmie laughs
at bumbled experiments in the lab, enjoys mistaken
explosions, thinks small fires liven up equations.
She tells Jimmie about the rigor with which Miss Turner
taught math, but how she made it seem transcendent.
When she complains of young people bent on trouble,
he teases, *I suppose you were a perfect student.*

She lifts an eyebrow the way her father did
to remind her of the use of silence, then lifts a corner
of her mouth to show she's ready for strong words.

Jimmie nods. *I hope I'm around when*
you find what seems worth fighting for.

Promises

Jimmie Goble and the other men who teach earn
more than the women, but only about half the salaries
of white teachers in Virginia. Jimmie paints houses
on weekends and vacations. He shyly tells her
he's putting away money for when he has a family.

Late one evening they walk in the hills,
where few lights swallow the Milky Way's pale splash.
The round moon has never seemed so close and golden.
She says, *Looking up, you can forget the world's problems.*

Jimmie sings, then opens his arm for them to dance
on the grass. *I'd give you the moon,* he whispers.
But if you wanted it, I know you'd just reach.

Love and History

The wedding is short and small. Katherine and Jimmie
want to keep the marriage quiet, since some schools
won't hire a wife they think should be content at home.
Katherine needs the salary and likes teaching,
though she's impatient when students ask,
Why should we study math?

Because it's amazing. Hearing the students laugh
as if she were joking, she tells them about jobs
in shops, offices, clinics. The equations she writes
on the blackboard aren't short, but there's never a need
to erase what's behind her to make room.

One day at the end of school she's surprised
to find the president of her old college waiting for her.
Dr. Davis explains that since new laws demand fair chances
for people of all races, he was asked to choose three people
likely to thrive in graduate school. *Dr. Claytor, Miss Turner,
and others boasted of you. Will you become one of the first
to integrate West Virginia University?*

Katherine tells Jimmie about the offer and scholarship, then says, *Of course I can't go. We just got married.*

You took a chance on me. Jimmie wraps his arms around her. *Why not take another one?*

What would I do with that degree? she asks him, then her parents. *Mama, I thought I'd be like you: teaching school, then raising children.*

But you're not just like me, Mama says. *I'll come help you settle in. West Virginia is quiet, but there's trouble farther south.*

Hope

Striding past white pillars into redbrick buildings,
Katherine stops at the classroom door,
gripping one of the math books given to her
by the principal of the school where she taught,
in case she's not allowed in the library.
She thinks of her mother waiting in a rented room
where she set up her sewing machine.

Then, for the first time in her life,
for one of the first times anywhere,
a woman enters an advanced math class
where every face but hers is white.

Unfinished Equations

As days pass, Katherine's grip on her books
loosens as she finds most people are friendly.
Professor Claytor prepared her well in calculus,
which lets her gracefully trace movements
between shifting points. She's at the top of the class,
where math means staying steady in the scatter and fog
of not knowing, where new ideas can be born.

Near the end of the semester, the scent of coffee
makes her queasy. Mama pours orange juice,
eyes the belt on Katherine's dress,
which she just let out a notch. *It looks like I'll need
to sew you some new dresses. And baby clothes.*

After Katherine finishes her classes, she tells
the principal at the school where she taught
that she won't come back or finish graduate school.
Keep the math books, he says.
You never know what will happen.

Three Daughters

As World War II begins, Katherine gives birth to a girl,
then another the next year, and a third as the war ends.
By the time Joylette, named after Katherine's mother,
can toddle across a room, little Constance
pulls herself up in the crib. By the time
Constance speaks short sentences,
the youngest girl, baby Katherine, can crawl.

Caring for small children is an experiment in time:
Days stretch. Months, then years,
collapse behind Katherine.
Every day is marked by discovery.
On Saturday mornings the girls play with dolls,
spin hula hoops in the backyard, look for lizards.
Jimmie makes paper kites and toy gliders
with balsa wood and rubber bands.
He shows their daughters how to angle their arms
and wrists when throwing and catching balls.

Katherine teaches school again, arranges violin lessons,
checks homework and Bible passages the girls memorize.

As the girls get older, she'll explain
Virginia's segregation laws, but for now,
she steers them to places where they'll be safe. Or almost.
When Joylette falls from a horse and crushes her mouth,
she learns which hospital will turn away
a girl with blood on her face because her skin is brown.

Again and again, Katherine tells her girls,
Look out for one another.
A single number isn't much. Math puts together many.
She brushes, divides, and braids their beautiful hair.
She wants them to know:
You're as good as anybody, but no better.

Frosting

Katherine and her sister stand among family
in a backyard talking about people they used to know.
I heard Miss Turner got married, Margaret says.
She moved north for a while to finish her PhD.

I'm happy for her. Katherine doesn't want
to be jealous, a rare pang.
She glances at her girls wearing crisp blue dresses.
Their folded white socks slip under their shiny black shoes
as they jump rope with cousins by the garage.
She takes Jimmie's elbow. They stroll
to the table with desserts. As he hands her
a slice of cake on a paper plate,
his brother-in-law joins them. Eric runs a community center
and knows a lot of people in and around Hampton,
where he says there are good jobs. *Some over at Langley
by the air base are open to women with math degrees.*

Katherine holds her fork over a slice of cake,
listens for her daughters jumping rope.
The two spinning and swishing ropes sound like many.

She says, *Moving might be hard on the girls.*
Our life is blessed the way it is.

Finish that cake. Jimmie scrapes up a dab of frosting
he holds to her lips. *It's time to take another chance.*

Another Road

Katherine and Jimmie pack the car.
The children bump against one another in the back.
Katherine remembers her father saying,
The world is bigger than this town. She turns
to Joylette, Constance, and Katherine,
asks, *Can you see the moon?*

Second Chances
HAMPTON, VIRGINIA, 1953

The girls go to Sunday school
at Carver Presbyterian Church, where Katherine joins
the choir. Jimmie takes a job
painting in the shipyard, which pays more than teaching.
Before leaving their new house, Katherine pulls on
cotton gloves and her church hat, twists around to check
that the seams in her stockings are straight.

Katherine is qualified for the job. After a desk opens
in the Langley Aeronautical Laboratory, she's welcomed
by Mrs. Dorothy Vaughan, who's worked here
since jobs opened to Black women during the war.
Now she's in charge of a dozen women called computers
who sit before clicking calculators
that cover almost half of each desk.
The women cheerfully check one another's math
and manners. No one must be late or untidy.
The hems of their skirts should be a proper length,
their hair smoothed or pinned down. Katherine knows
that if fault is found with one, they'll all look bad.

Changing Course

Katherine's work is fast and flawless.
Soon Dorothy tells her, *The director of the flight research*
division asked me to send my best mathematician
for a job that will take two weeks.

I haven't been here much longer than that.
Katherine glances around at the women she talks
with at lunch about the new shirts that need
less ironing, what each plans to cook for supper.

I've never seen anyone work through numbers as quickly
as you, Dorothy says. *And we've got a superior group here,*
all with college math degrees. The white women
can keep data straight, but those computers don't have
the education to see past what they're told.
The research scientists come to our room for help.

Katherine picks up her handbag, says good-bye,
walks to another building. At the door to a big room,
she counts fifteen white men, three white women,
and one woman the same color as her.

On the chalkboard, she spots an equation grown too long
for paper. She swiftly follows its length and turns,
hears a quiet call to what's yet to be known.

An Invitation

Men wearing rumpled white shirts hand Katherine
equations to solve, some stretching ten pages deep.
She charts a plane's speed and height over the course
of a flight, figuring in gusts and vibrations,
particularly during dangerous descents, looking
for ways to keep planes in the air during wild winds.

She bends into work she was meant to do.
The men around her seem to recognize the posture.
Most care about math's certainty, not looking back,
but forward to a time of faster flights.

She goes to the hall, walks past rooms of white researchers.
A bathroom door with a sign
that says WOMEN implies white women.
It's meant to keep her out, the way Virginia laws
ban her from libraries, parts of buses,
lunch counters, and movie theaters.
Katherine doesn't see a COLORED WOMEN sign in this building
where she has work to do and no time to waste looking
for a bathroom when there's one right here for women.

Unsaid

Late one afternoon, the man with a desk by Katherine's
asks where she came from. She and Ted Skopinksi talk
about the West Virginia mountains they both miss.
After she's been there three months, they start work
together on a paper. He lends her copies of *Aviation Week*.
Overhead lights whir, bright on men too intent
on their work to pay much mind to their own skin and hair,
never mind hers. They care about her equations,
which explore what happens as a plane's
particular shape and weight roughen the air.

As planes fly faster, the math gets more complicated.
Katherine prepares charts
for meetings women aren't allowed to attend.
She signs papers to keep her work secret,
though she can't think of anyone outside this building
who would care about her charts.
When she goes to the grocery store or church,
friends ask, *How's your family?* not, *How is work?*

She eats lunch at her desk, which saves time, money,
and worry about what table at the cafeteria to sit at.

Often the men eat sandwiches too, playing cards
or talking with her about equations that start small,
then sprawl to show how far someone may go.
No one mentions how their children go to different schools
or asks, *How's Jimmie?* She's glad because the sound
of his name might unstitch her composed face.
She's taken on enough firsts,
doesn't want to be the first to cry in this room.

She won't use words like "headaches" or "hospital."
Or confide how Jimmie has recently missed
work in the shipyard, stopped telling jokes,
though he can work up a grin for their daughters.
She doesn't want to talk about neighbors and cousins
who quietly bring casseroles and care.
She'd rather talk about flight, turbulence,
waves of wind behind wings.

Clouds

Every Sunday morning, Katherine stands and sways
with the choir. She sings *Glory, glory, glory,*
stretches the syllables of *Hallelujah.*
But one day she sits in a front pew instead of with the choir,
as they sing about rain, rivers, and going home.

The preacher speaks of Jimmie's pride in his wife
and the three girls who lean against her,
smelling of starch. Katherine can't remember
who ironed their dresses and ribbons, braided their hair,
polished their patent leather shoes. Had she managed?

The preacher calls out words the congregation calls back.
Then Katherine leaves the pew with people's eyes on her,
like a bride walking the wrong way.
Friends gather around outside. One hands her
a cup of coffee she doesn't want, but finally sips.
It's cold. She touches her daughters' hair. Tomorrow,
as impossible as it seems, she'll fix them breakfast.

Chesapeake Bay

That Christmas, crumpled tissues are strewn
among the gift wrap.
But after the holidays, Katherine says it's time
to get back to work and school as usual.
After supper one night, the girls gather around
the linoleum-topped table
under a bright lamp that hums like bees.
Joylette slams shut her math book. *I can't do this.*

Everybody says that. It's almost never true, Katherine says.
If you work hard, you can do whatever you want.

Mom, *that doesn't always happen.*

You're right. Katherine touches Joylette's hand.
Tomorrow, let's go walk by the water.

She packs supper in a basket and drives to the bay.
Her youngest girl tosses stones to see how far
they'll skip. Above them, dark birds soar, wings wide.

Opening a Door

When Langley becomes part of NASA, the workers
focus less on trying to increase the speed
and safety of jet planes and more on a mission
to send a spacecraft around the earth.

Katherine works with Ted Skopinksi until he's needed
elsewhere. She keeps on exploring the angles formed
by a point on the rotating earth, the North Pole,
and land that might be just below a moving spacecraft.
Euler's formula guides her as she fills in distances
between the known points of slopes and possibilities.
She writes papers, but her name is taken off the top.

When men return from meetings, she asks
questions that could take her deeper into problems
they can't answer. She asks, *Why can't I go to the meetings?*

Her boss sighs. *It's just how it's done.*

Is there a law against it?

He shakes his head.
She doesn't stop asking
until he finally says,
All right. Go.

Turn Around

Katherine meets Jim Johnson in the choir loft.
His river-deep voice joins hers singing,
"His Eye Is on the Sparrow." After services they talk,
then more at church suppers and a picnic,
where he tells her about his past. *I fixed navy planes*
to make sure pilots were safe in the sky.
Then I signed on for the war in Korea.
I got to see a lot of the world,
but now I'm ready to stay in one place.
I'm glad for a good job at the post office and joined
the army reserves. But tell me about your work.

They stroll to a field where friends play baseball.
Watching someone swing a bat,
the ball rising and curving back down,
Katherine explains how she's trying to figure out
how a spacecraft might soar past the atmosphere.

Before long she invites Jim to join her family at suppers.
He doesn't tell jokes the way the girls' father had,
but they appreciate his tender attention to their tastes

in music and meals. Just as he was content to repair planes
rather than fly them, he wants to fit in here: watching,
listening, seeing what's needed but not pushing change.

Sometimes Jim meets Katherine at work,
bringing sandwiches they share on the steps,
watching the moon rise.
He says, *I'm a lucky guy to find a beautiful, smart woman*
and three girls as great as their mother.

We're set in our ways, she says, but smiles.

Good ways. I'd be honored to be part of them.
From his pocket, he pulls a ring
she doesn't hesitate to slip on.

Her Name

After she marries and becomes Katherine Johnson,
she calculates a flight path from liftoff, around the earth,
to splashdown. She works backward,
starting with the part of the ocean where the capsule
is meant to land. She hands her boss a report
thick with charts, tables, and references
she checked and checked again.
She says, My name belongs on this paper.

The thirty-four-page report with twenty-two crucial
equations becomes the first paper in her division
with a woman's name at the top.

Seen and Unseen

Katherine flips through newspapers and magazines
that show pictures of seven men who each hope
to be the first American to soar into space.
They work at Cape Canaveral in Florida,
where rockets will launch,
but come to Langley to take engineering classes
and train in models of capsules.
Katherine sees them pass through the corridors
with their close-cut hair and pale pink faces,
their pace swingier than most here.
All were military test pilots, used to danger,
taking orders, and making decisions
at a moment's notice. The aspiring astronauts
are strong and serene, but when one goes into space,
he will be as vulnerable as a baby, packed
into a capsule with barely room to move his elbows.

Katherine's data sheets grow longer and wider.
Some of the smallest numbers
stand for the biggest possibilities.
How will the rocket rise to the edge of the atmosphere

and release a capsule that escapes the pull of gravity?
Can it withstand the heat made by friction
moving at eighteen thousand miles per hour.
Her calculations must guide the capsule
around the earth, which isn't a perfect sphere,
but bulges in the middle and turns a bit differently each day.

She honors both change and the way the world
reminds her of the glory of repetition.
"Hallelujah" is rarely sung just once.

Trust

John Glenn, who treats the flag, his family, and women
with respect, is chosen for this space voyage.
Shortly before liftoff, he learns that the course
of his flight comes from electronic computers.
He's long flown airplanes and loves machines,
but there was always a person at the controls.
In space he could live or die, and can't trust
a noisy machine the way he can a human
with a heart and mind. He says,
Get the girl to check the numbers.

The printouts from a new electronic computer
that fills and heats up a room are rushed to Katherine.
She stays up late, grips her pencil hard, reaching
far past decimal points to make sure every digit matches
those in long lists shuffled from computers.
She is both as calm and as terrified as a pilot.
Any slight lapse of her attention
might mean the capsule could sink in the sea,
the nation's hero too far away to be found.

Orbits

Katherine stands with colleagues between screens,
charts, and maps. On February 20, 1962, the results
of their work will astonish
more than a hundred million viewers.
Her heart flutters as they watch the rocket tremble
and soar past smoke. *Godspeed, John Glenn.*

Katherine says a silent prayer.
Her eyes stay on the television showing
the suited-up astronaut surrounded by switches,
gauges, and panels knit with steel and math.
As the capsule begins to orbit, John Glenn's voice
breaks over the radio. He marvels at the curving line
of the African coast, wind blowing desert sand into waves,
snow-covered mountains, a view he could cover
with his hand. He speaks of the deep green sea,
the spit and spark of a thunderstorm,
says the state of Florida *looks just like it does on a map.*

After the first orbit, the capsule wobbles.
John Glenn overrules the computers to keep

the spacecraft steady and on course.
Then a safety light clicks on.

The heat shield is loose. A scientist chokes on his words.
No one around Katherine needs to say what they all know:
If that shield tears off, the *Friendship 7*
could burn almost as hot as the sun,
turn to flame as it falls back to earth.

Meanwhile, John Glenn circles the earth again
and again, seeing the sun rise and set
three times in less than five hours.
The spacecraft hurtles down as planned.
Katherine breathes easily until screens go blank.
She hears a snap and static
before sounds stop from the capsule.
Whatever is happening isn't supposed to happen.

Her breath snags. She stands among people
who made decisions about every wire
looped around the man cocooned in the capsule.

Friends hide their faces as the silence
from the falling capsule drags through four minutes
and twenty seconds, enough time for her to hear
a whole song about rivers and rain hum through her mind.
Then everyone looks up at the sound
of static. The astronaut says, *That was a real fireball.*

Flames flickered around the spacecraft,
but guided by the math Katherine worked on,
it now spins safely into the sea.
Waves lap around the bobbing capsule
as John Glenn opens the door and grins.
Katherine adds her voice to the room loud with cheers.

For the first time all year, she leaves work
before sundown. She drives to the coast
to face earth's shadow, a blue band that briefly widens
as an edge of the world slips into beautiful darkness.

Reaching Higher

Now that an American has soared around the world,
President Kennedy wants one to fly to the moon.
Katherine calculates the speed and direction
of both a rocket and the earth's spin.
She analyzes how much force will be made by the rocket,
how momentum will build as it pushes past the pull
of the earth's gravity. She and colleagues write long reports,
including pages that begin with *What if . . . ?*
She charts the stars in case the electricity or computers fail
and the astronauts must find their way back
the way sailors once did, guided by constellations.

Reaching the moon seems impossible.
But every day, Katherine works with people
who mean to make that happen. One number at a time.

Dreams

Filled with her mother's faith in her, Joylette goes to college
across town at Hampton, famous for the old oak tree
where President Lincoln's Emancipation Proclamation
was read for the first time in the South,
declaring that all held as slaves
be henceforward forever free.
Soon a school for them was founded by the tree.

For about a hundred years the Hampton campus
has been quiet, but now students march through town,
demanding that promises of equality finally be kept.
Friends from church tell Katherine about students
who bring homework to the five-and-dime store,
open books on the lunch counter, and pretend to study.
Some are shoved from their seats.
Angry white people knock cups and plates off the counter.
The students get up, wipe up spilled mustard and coffee,
return to their task. Others stage sit-ins at libraries.

When Joylette talks about joining a march for justice,
Katherine shakes her head. *I just want you to be safe.*

If they put you in jail,
you won't ever get that job you want at NASA.
It won't matter that you were marching peacefully.

Joylette touches the corner of her mouth,
which had been cut when she was a child turned away
from a hospital with blood on her brown face.
She won't promise she won't protest,
but stands strong as the oak tree
where people gather again with new hope.

Borderless

With math as powerful and soundless as the hands
of a choir director silently shaping music,
Katherine measures arcs between a spot on the moon
that's eleven miles long and three miles wide
and what was Cape Canaveral,
renamed Cape Kennedy after the death of a president
whose dreams shape their work.
While one astronaut pilots around the moon,
two others will take a smaller craft to the surface,
which looks pockmarked and silver-gray.
Katherine works out the crucial part
where the two vehicles meet at just the right time.

After years of work, she and millions of others
watch television to see Neil Armstrong, Buzz Aldrin,
and Michael Collins fly to the moon.
Two astronauts ride the *Eagle* module to the surface.
They stir dust as they lumber and bob,
taking close-up photos of craters and long-distance photos
of the blue-marbled world, whole and undivided as the sky.

Unhidden

After the astronauts fly safely home,
Katherine works on ways to reach Mars, a journey
that may uncover more history hidden in darkness.
After thirty-three years at Langley, she retires,
but she doesn't stop asking questions.

She's proud of her daughters' work teaching
and raising children,
Joylette's career as a NASA mathematician.
Katherine adds photographs of her grandchildren,
then her great-grandchildren, on a table by a phone
she answers one afternoon. Margot Lee Shetterly
tells her that her father was a research scientist at Langley.
She speaks of her childhood singing in a church
filled with mathematicians, reciting Bible verses
to a Sunday school teacher who was retired from Langley.
Now Margot is a writer and back
in Hampton with questions.
Did you love math as a child? she asks Katherine.
Who helped you along? Who stood in your way?

Katherine talks about herself, insists, *I just did my share*.
She speaks of how she worked with Dorothy Vaughan,
Mary Jackson, and Christine Darden,
all Black women who once taught math.
Katherine checked her work against computer programs
written by Dr. Evelyn Boyd Granville, one of the first
African American women to earn a PhD in mathematics.
Katherine used NASA's planetary flight handbook,
partially written by Mary Golda Ross, a Cherokee woman
who became the first woman engineer at Lockheed,
where she designed satellites and rockets.
Working around the same time, Amy Gonzales,
a Mexican American, calculated rocket trajectories.

Sometimes alone, often together,
women opened doors to mystery. None expected
to be celebrated beyond the walls where they worked.

But at ninety-eight, Katherine Johnson,
resplendent in silver and pearls
at a premiere of the movie *Hidden Figures*,
graciously nods as people stand to applaud her.
Fame is built with math, rides on an arc.

Shine on one point shows up others.
Katherine won't forget those who didn't live to see
their own brilliance praised. She cares more
about getting things right
than clapping, which goes on and on.
The world has long waited to cheer
for a woman who did her best, and was extraordinary.

MAKING CHANGE WITH CHARTS, PART II

✦

EDNA LEE PAISANO

(1948–2014)

Beginnings
NEZ PERCE COUNTY, IDAHO, 1955

Pretending to be a wild horse, Edna runs
past canyons and camas flowers blue as the sky.
She picks huckleberries and swims in the river
with cousins. They warm up by a campfire,
where their grandfather fries fish he caught.

Grandmother layers a pit with hot stones
to roast camas bulbs tucked in cloth and leaves.
The smallest cousin rolls on her back,
clutching a bag of marshmallows, laughing
as she doles them out to toast over the fire.
Edna counts stars until the sky is filled
with almost as much shine as darkness.

Art and Math

Trust me, Grandmother says, demanding precision
as Edna counts colored beads for moccasins.
Stitch by stich, the single beads shape themselves
into triangles, rectangles, trapezoids, and rhombuses.
Some rows are jagged at the top, like the bar graphs
she loves making to compare sales
of milk or baskets of corn, radishes, and hot peppers
from one year to the next.
Edna asks, *Did your grandmother teach you how to sew?*

No. Grandmother tells her about the government school
she attended far from home. Children were forbidden
to use their first language, ordered to speak only English.
Lessons were meant to whittle away memory
or respect for their family's customs.
But I came back here and taught your mother and aunts.

When Edna vows never to leave, Grandmother says,
Not until you go to college, like your parents.
Edna knows they met in one. Her mother returned

with her father, who still misses
the Pueblo of Laguna foothills.
Edna sorts blue, yellow, and red beads, stitches
so lightning bolts and wild roses rise into view.

A Girl's Education

Wooden rulers clatter as students draw
straight lines for words to ride on.
Edna stacks numbers as carefully as kindling.
Sometimes they flicker like sparks that can't be caught,
but snag in the airy net of guessing.

In this school, no language is called wrong, but math,
with its bent toward equality, is Edna's favorite.
Math shows no favor for the past or future,
but builds a home where she breathes.

A bell rings. Small children spray from the shut door,
shriek and sprint across the playground.
Edna is also gleeful that she can work inside or out.
Near home, she draws crisscrossing lines in the dirt.
Her cousins toss stones over the grid.
If a stone falls in one square, she wonders,
what are the chances it will land there again?
Estimates and probability are also her subjects
as she counts clouds, watches grasses bend,
looks for birds and listens to insects to predict weather
later in the day. One small sign can stretch far.

Sold

Edna's mother teaches school. Her father works
in the lumberyard. They're both busy at their farm
on weekends, when Edna and her grandmother
arrange beaded bags and moccasins
on a table in town. Vans and station wagons
with out-of-state license plates stop.

Grandmother seems smaller here than at home.
When asked questions, the corners of her eyes and mouth
pinch tight as the end of a pulled thread.
Edna's face warms, slightly embarrassed
by her grandmother's polite but short replies,
her refusal to put at ease tourists who look
as if they expect more than moccasins.
Maybe forgiveness, though Grandmother told Edna
not to blame the living for the invisible borders that
drivers passed on their way into the reservation.
One woman asks Edna, *Do you go to school?*

Yes. Edna smiles though the question seems silly.
Doesn't she know today is Saturday?

When asked, *What's your favorite subject?*
Edna says, *Math.* She's twelve now
but remembers the thrill when she first opened a book
with that word on the cover, replacing arithmetic.
She's always ready to talk about her love for breaking
equations into parts, putting them back together,
but the woman has turned away.

Maybe Grandmother is right.
Strangers don't want their stories.

Seventeen

Edna runs her hand over her damp dark hair,
which smells of the clear river that rolls around rocks.
Has the water already forgotten the shape
she makes when swimming?

Life here is hard, Grandmother says.
*We need more and better jobs. Not everyone
comes back.* She gives Edna a dress she sewed
with fringe and tassels, like those worn by ancestors.
Edna won't wear it at college or maybe anywhere,
but the deerskin is a promise that she belongs.

Here and Beyond

Mathematics is a mirror. In college,
equations make Edna certain of who she is.
But she'd be ashamed to just follow
what she loves and not give back. She's here
thanks to money from her parents, grandparents,
tribe, and country. She can't return
to the reservation and say, *I'm a mathematician.*

She puts away her slide rule, protractor,
the compass she used to draw and measure circles,
along with her beading.
Training to be a teacher, she reads books,
passes out pencils and paper, helps children
stack blocks into buildings and bridges.

Each hurt and hungry child who gathers around her knees
teaches her about the needs of those beyond this circle.
One day she takes out her tools again.
Earning a master's in social work in Seattle,
she translates stories of people in peril to numbers,

then unfolds these back to words.
She studies laws that, like multiplication,
could make changes not just for one child but many.
She draws rose diagrams, coxcomb graphs,
and charts that compare children who eat healthy food
to those who are hungry. She contrasts the chances
of children who have books in their homes with those
likely to hear fewer words or know the shapes of stories,
factoring in how not all stories come from paper.
Those deprived of food and books have a hard time
in school and are less likely to go to college.
Math works out ways to give everyone a fair chance,
nudges one example to fan out past paper.

Multiplication
WASHINGTON, DC, 1972

Three years ago, intricate math helped two astronauts walk
on the moon and get safely back to Earth.
Now Edna works with a calculator that fits in her hand,
hears talk of computers that might fit on a lap
instead of a floor.
This seems far-fetched, but it's a time of change and hope.
The nation's capital is often alive with protests,
including marches for equality in schools
no longer segregated, but not yet fair.
New laws are passed.
Title IX brings new chances for girls and women.

Still, the people who first lived on this continent
often seem forgotten. Some celebrate Native Americans
of long ago, while looking past the living.
We're here, Edna wants to say with her work,
and crosses the country for a job with Head Start.
She means to make sure that Native American children
have breakfasts, blocks, and good books,
not in just one home or school, but across the nation.

She works hard, tries to ignore the way aches
in her shoulders and legs come, go, then last longer.
Her ankles swell and stiffen, making it hard to walk to work.
She misses the canyons and big sky,
but likes the capital's white buildings,
with straight and unbending pillars,
doorways and windows symmetrical as sunflowers.
Stone stairs are numbered with intention.

Challenges

Edna fights a fever and deep fatigue to finish work.
Her pencil falls from her hands.
She wills pain to stay in one place,
like the point of her compass. But illness sets its own course.
As she pushes herself up from a green wicker chair,
her knees feel like knots that refuse to loosen.
Her doctor says she has rheumatoid arthritis
and must find ways to cope with pain
that will always be her partner.

The future is like a river bound to shift to different speeds.
Edna makes plans while bracing for surprises.
Washington, DC, gives her ways to live with less walking.
The Potomac River is murky, but her shoulders are soothed
at a gym, where she swims laps in a turquoise-colored pool.

Silences

Edna's grace with numbers lands her a job at the
US Census Bureau, where she's the first Native American
to work full-time. She studies measurements
of people's strength, health, and wealth,
balances ratios of true and false,
subtracts because paring shows patterns.
Numbers trim toward truth. She lays them like bricks,
straight and side by side. Starting with certainty,
she moves through the unpredictable,
then lands on a certain but wider space.
Edna makes records of the present
to learn what will be wanted in coming years.
She doesn't need all the information,
but the right information, and to recognize
when more is crucial and then find it.

Numbers can show stories hidden like knots under cloth.
Seeing some meant to show
the population of Idaho towns,
she's stunned to find listed only about half of those
who live in her old town. She tells colleagues,

Many citizens of the Nez Perce nation
are missing from these papers.

That may be true in other reservations.
A man at the desk by hers nods. *We just mean to help,*
but some American Indians won't answer
our questions and get left out.

Edna looks down at her shoes, remembers
her grandmother's butter-thick silences
when tourists looked over moccasins
that mean one thing to people who stitch them
and another to those who buy them.
Some Indians learned to hide what they loved
so it wouldn't be taken.
Some hesitate to say even their names.

I'll write new questions. Edna understands
that tucking stories behind silence or slanting sentences
has given census workers the wrong numbers,
kept families like hers from their fair share
of help for building schools, hospitals, and roads.
Words and numbers may be gifts or tools for theft,
used to bring together or push apart.

True and False

Edna sets a blue clay mug and a cheese sandwich
on her desk, examines old questions.
Some pierce. Others are walls.
Are you an American Indian?
has more complicated answers than *Yes* or *No*.
Census workers used to decide someone's race
or ancestry based on how they looked or where they lived.
Now they ask, *What do you call yourself?*
and make room for more than one choice.
The coming 1980 census will be the first time
no one will be asked to name *the head of the family*.
As if just one person should be in charge.

Edna writes questions she wants asked by people
who are more like those whose homes they may enter,
who see and hear differently than outsiders
shaped by old tales of tepees, arrows, and feathers.
She needs numbers that more truly reflect people living
in or outside reservations, in small towns or cities.
Families are more like cloth than furniture,
their boundaries not as solid as wood.

Homes

Edna runs her hand over her straight black hair,
which smells faintly of chlorine from the pool.
She tries to ignore the pain in her knees
as she puts a pot of blue flowers on her desk,
though none are the shade of the sky on a day
so fine the river catches color from above.

Learning of her grandmother's death, she holds
the deerskin dress to her face, breathes the scent
of home. She bakes potatoes and carrots,
but nothing matches the sweet and smoky taste
of camas bulbs pulled from a stone-lined pit.
She misses the sound of horses galloping past canyons,
the scent of wild roses under a sky unsplit by monuments.

Taking Measure

Edna studies people and where they live
within borders that change as much as rivers,
mountain ridges, and their names.
County lines, state lines, and power lines
can duck in and out of sight.
Old maps noted the numbers of footsteps
between markers of rocks or twisted trees.
But the boundaries of reservations
show how history is written with division.
The calculations of how much land should be left
to those who first lived there didn't factor in much fairness.

Edna's numbers break the world into parts
she patches back together.
Her columns are straight as the spine of a book
before covers open to spill stories.
Over years of work, she opens paths
through layers of data
from hundreds of tribes, each
with its own way of keeping triumphs and sorrows.

Her charts and graphs are not meant for a queen,
but to convince busy people who work
with the president
of the need for reform.
The government often underestimated the numbers
of the peoples who first lived on this land rich
with possibilities before being forced onto reservations.

Edna's tallies show the Nez Perce population
in many Idaho towns is more than twice
what was shown in the last census.
Much of the American Indian population
looks larger than it was ten years ago. Some changes
are due to healthier babies and people living longer,
but new statistics reflect more truth.

Edna Lee Paisano's work means some schools
will get more books. More children will eat breakfast,
more homes will be built, so bedrooms won't be crowded.
She's proud. Some joys are impossible to count.
Still, math breaks open new views,
shows a spiraling way toward home.

Blue Again

Silver-gray runs through strands of Edna's hair.
She leans on a cane, watching children run
through fields blue with star-shaped flowers.
She brings home charts the way others carry cakes
or handmade clothing. Good gifts change shapes,
make a circle. She left here thinking she couldn't return
as a mathematician. She returns to tell children
how math can help them find jobs with computers
or in business or places no one can yet see.

Edna's knees ache, but she slowly kneels
to dig up camas bulbs that she roasts in a pit,
tastes sweetness she never forgot.
She takes off her shoes to wade in the river
that rolls around rocks. The river remembers her shape.

LOOKING BEYOND

✦

VERA RUBIN

(1928–2016)

Still Awake
WASHINGTON, DC, 1938

Vera opens the bedroom window, wonders
how long stars have been shining,
if her sister, sleeping across the invisible line
they set in their bed, is dreaming. She wonders
if anyone else in the neighborhood is still awake,
why night makes her thirsty,
and where questions come from.

At last she shuts her eyes,
tucks her black-speckled notebook under her pillow,
which smells of backyard air and grass.
She dozes on the spinning earth, wakes,
finds familiar stars in new parts of the sky.
Darkness makes much disappear, but also reveals.

The Library Book

The cover shows a silhouette of a girl in a long dress
and bonnet peering through a telescope.
Vera reads about the Quaker girl who lived on an island
where her father recorded the movement of stars
to help sailors find their way. Maria Mitchell
became the first American to discover a comet,
made of dust, rock, and ice that heats up near the sun,
and streaks the sky with brief shine. As Vera reads,
her breath rises, falls, opens with a parachute's grace.

Table Manners

In sixth-grade math class, Vera becomes friends with a girl
whose light hair is as straight as her own dark hair is curly.
Jane's right front tooth was chipped
when she fell from a tree.
After Vera shows her the star maps
in her speckled notebook,
Jane searches for graph paper in her father's desk.
She finds a protractor and slide rule that they experiment
with when Jane's mother invites Vera to stay for supper.
In the middle of the meal, she asks,
How was school? Vera, what's your favorite subject?

Math, she replies.

I was terrible at math. Jane's mother laughs lightly,
unembarrassed, almost proud.
Jane's brother wrinkles his nose. *Yuck. I hate arithmetic.*

No one scolds or urges the boy to give numbers a chance,
the way his father praises vegetables
as the little boy hides peas under mashed potatoes.

Vera doesn't suppose anyone means to be unkind.
But she's stung by how they suggest what she loves
is odd, unworthy, inexplicable.

She glances at Jane, who looks down at her plate.
Doesn't anyone in her family know
math is Jane's favorite subject too?

Questions

Vera and Jane are fourteen when they measure poles
and blankets to put up a tent in the backyard.
They stash number puzzles, flashlights, books,
and grape jelly sandwiches her mother packed
in case they get hungry in the middle of the night.

A gust of wind collapses the tent.
The girls crawl out and lie on their backs,
listening to crickets and traffic, fanning out their fingers
to measure distances between stars.
Vera asks, *Do you think we could make a telescope?*

We had a big tube that held the linoleum
my dad put on the kitchen floor, Jane says.
Their voices sound louder in the dark.

They can't find that tube, but they ride the bus
downtown to a flooring store and get one for free.
Vera's father helps her build a telescope
with pipes and plumbing fittings,
lenses, an old bottle cap, and a bit of paint.

As they wield tools, he tells her about when he was a boy
called Pesach Kobchefski, before coming to this country
where his name was changed to Philip Cooper.
These memories seem as precious and faraway as stars.

The telescope doesn't work as well as Vera hoped.
But night holds questions as beautiful
as those in math class. She likes the sprawling uncertainty
as well as the ends of complicated equations.

Laws of Gravity

Vera's algebra teacher finds mistakes as intriguing
as right answers. Mr. Gilbert's curiosity
makes Vera eager to take physics in a room with cabinets
filled with scales and parts of old radios and generators.
There, she and Jane are the only girls among boys
who often seem giddy, as if after years of sharing
about half the classroom with girls, they landed
in a special league. They laugh at the teacher's jokes
about explosions, Bunsen burner tragedies,
and mysteries under the hoods of cars.

Vera listens as Mr. Himes tosses an apple,
watches it fall, and talks about how the sun's gravity
holds together the solar system.
Mercury, *the planet closest to the sun, moves fastest.*
The farther a planet is from the sun, the slower its orbit.

Mr. Himes praises more of Newton's discoveries,
Pythagoras's theory, the way Galileo showed
the earth revolves around the sun, and Einstein's ideas
about time and space. Mr. Himes says, *Lesser insights*

come from sheer hard work. *Madame Curie stirred*
pitchblende for years to reduce it to radium.
It's the first time he's mentioned a woman scientist. *If*
she hadn't discovered that element, someone else would have.

But how did Mare Curie suspect something wild
was in the ore? Vera raises her hand as a boy blurts out,
Didn't her husband do most of the thinking?

As other boys laugh, Vera lowers her hand.
She won't point out the genius it took to discover
that stone dug from the earth holds secrets of star shine.
Will the boys snicker or think she's showing off
if she says that after Pierre died, Marie became
the first person to receive two Nobel Prizes,
the second for her work alone?

In the Cafeteria

As Vera opens her brown paper bag,
Jane says, *I got a C minus on the precalculus test.*
That's almost a D. Maybe
I shouldn't study math in college after all.

But *you love it,* Vera says. *That was a terrible test.*
One boy near me got mad at his bad grade.
Another got paler than usual and swallowed hard.
But I didn't hear them give up their dreams.

Jane shrugs, nods toward a girl who's popular, pretty, rich.
I wish I were her. Who would you be if you could be anyone?

Vera is shocked, silent. She looks down
at the dress she sewed from cloth
printed with cherries that looked good rolled up
in the store but seems silly on a person.
The stitches in the hem are too wide.
She makes mistakes but wouldn't swap who she is:
the girl who built a rough telescope with her father,
who helped a friend make a tent,

even if it toppled in the wind.
She wouldn't want to lose even the girl
who was silent when boys laughed about Marie Curie.
Someday she might be more brave.

Listening

An adviser visiting Vera's high school talks with her
about college. *I don't believe any girls major in astronomy.*
She glances at Vera's record. *I see you do well
in French, sing in the glee club, and enjoy art.
Perhaps you could paint astronomical scenes.*

Vera remembers the library book about Maria Mitchell,
the first woman to teach astronomy at Vassar College.
Vera applies there. After learning she was accepted,
she spots her physics teacher in the hall.
Her words tumble: *I got a scholarship to Vassar College!*

Stay away from science and you should do okay.
Mr. Himes smiles.

Vera catches her breath. Has he forgotten
she earns all As? Just two girls take the class.
Does he even know which one she is?

Starting Out
POUGHKEEPSIE, NEW YORK, 1944

In the all-women's college, girls who were quiet
among boys in high school now wave their hands
to ask questions, interrupt, argue about ideas.
Professor Maud Makemson teaches the secrets
of differential equations, which break long problems,
and integral equations, which put the pieces back together.
Calculus mirrors the swift changes of stars.

Vera uses chalk on black paper to draw the orbital
patterns of asteroids, some discovered by her professor.
Science unfolds new stories, while math helps
turn the pages, touches the past, reaches
for the future, makes room for uncertainty.

The Motion of Stars

Home for the summer, Vera agrees to meet
the son of a couple her parents know at the synagogue.
No one told her how handsome he is.
Bob Rubin is dark-haired, a little taller than her.
As they stroll after a concert, they talk
about music and gravity. Vera looks up at stars
that are born and die in clouds of dust.
She says, *It's amazing that all the stars*
we see belong to our Milky Way.

It's good to meet someone who recognizes
what's in the sky as more than names for candy bars,
cereal, and cars. Bob tells her a bit
about his war work, doing research for the navy,
while studying physics in graduate school at Cornell.
I want to follow the biggest questions I can think up.

When I was growing up, I leaned on the windowsill,
slept, then woke up to find the stars in new places,
she says. *I'm still curious about those movements of stars*
and the earth. Old questions matter too.

Autumn

Dipping graham crackers in milk or munching on apples,
Vera works on math that reflects forces on paper
and sometimes suggests other powers that cannot be seen.
She helps a friend with homework.
Alice puts down her pencil and complains,
*I thought astronomy would be easier
than other sciences, but there's so much math.
And Professor Makemson is weird. What are those charms
and stone carvings doing in the observatory?*

She researched astronomy and religion in China and Egypt,
Vera says. *And won a Guggenheim fellowship
to study Mayan astronomy.*

*Whatever that is. Tell me more about the boy
who takes the trolley to visit you here on weekends.
I hope you'll invite me to the wedding.*

He doesn't visit every weekend. Vera blushes. *And I don't know
about marriage. I want to keep studying astronomy.*

You can't do both, Alice says. You can be like Miss Mitchell,
who never married, or be a wife and mother.
Professor Makemson has children,
but she got divorced. A woman has to choose.

The Old Globe

Her last year in college, Vera is the only astronomy major.
She has a job in the observatory as clock winder,
telescope keeper, and paper grader. Under the dome,
arced as the sky seems to be, she likes
using the telescopes almost whenever she pleases.
But it's odd to be the only person in some classes
that Professor Makemson says were filled
back when Maria Mitchell taught.
In 1869, right after graduation, six majors took a train
to Ohio to observe the total eclipse of the sun.
The professor's voice echoes under the dome.
It may have been the first all-woman scientific expedition.

That's history. I care about what no one knows.
Vera looks at the marble bust of a serious woman
with her hair worn in ringlets.

Scientists should know who came before them.
It's a hundred years since Maria Mitchell's comet discovery.
and there's no notice even here,
where she taught for twenty years.

Maud Makemson picks up an old celestial globe
from a table covered with star charts and stones.
This was going to be thrown away,
but I thought you might want it.

The globe, its surface wrinkled with age,
feels heavy in Vera's hands. She's uncertain
what this history has to do with her, but grateful
for her professor's vision of her as an astronomer.
She thinks she loves Bob but needs to tell him
she's not ready to stop asking questions about galaxies.

On her way out of the observatory, Vera winds her scarf
around the marble bust of Maria Mitchell.
Maybe Professor Makemson is right.
Women pioneers in science and math deserve more respect.

Back Roads

One weekend walking past woods, Vera tells Bob,
Princeton won't take women, but I applied to Harvard
for graduate school. They have good telescopes.

He nods. *You should go to the best university.*

If Bob hadn't wanted her to go to wherever
she chose, she might not have said that she could learn
anywhere, might not have applied to Cornell.
His proposal isn't like a math problem
for which she has to consider a series of what-ifs.
Vera doesn't hesitate before saying yes.

The Wedding

After the crack of purposely shattered glass,
cries of *Mazel tov*, and wishes for many children,
Vera and Bob Rubin hold hands as darkness comes,
vow to keep room for both science and religion.
Stars within galaxies change, and galaxies
within clusters change, and clusters of galaxies
change within the universe. The sky is one wide road.

The Motion of Galaxies
ITHACA, NEW YORK, 1949

The head of the astronomy department greets Vera, saying,
There aren't many jobs in astronomy. Don't expect to get one.
She'd hoped for a warmer welcome, but other professors
support her studies of movements in 109 spiral galaxies.
She charts star speeds and directions,
measures how each shrinks or grows,
writes equations that sprawl and tangle
into brief certainty, then back to wonder:
Does the universe rotate
the way planets move around the sun?

While she works toward a master's degree in astronomy,
Bob continues studying for a PhD in physics.
In the evenings, at the kitchen table,
on the sofa, or in bed, they talk
about raccoons prowling the neighborhood,
the age of the milk in the refrigerator, and the cosmos.
As Vera cleans her glasses, spreads papers
under a green-shaded lamp, Bob teases her about the way
she tilts her head when a problem confounds her.

After just over a year of marriage, Vera's skin feels tender.
She's tired. She counts back weeks,
then the months ahead, eager to complete her paper
about the rotation of galaxies before giving birth.

Hers

The head of the astronomy department reads Vera's thesis,
says, *Some of your research looks sloppy, but*
it might be discussed at the American Astronomical Society.
Professor Shaw glances at Vera's arcing belly.
I'll read it and use my name, since I'm a member.

If you think people will be interested, I'll go,
Vera says. *And read my paper under my own name.*

What One Young Mother Finds

Vera and Bob don't own a car, but her parents offer
to drive them from Ithaca with their three-week-old boy,
who's gorgeous and complicated as a galaxy.
Vera loves the way the baby seems knowable
in the moment but holds secrets inside.

Thick snow blows over the sedan her father
sometimes pulls over to scrape ice off the windshield.
The heater clatters and clangs. As the car skids,
Vera tightens her grip on the baby on her lap.

Your father escaped from anti-Semitic thugs in Poland,
Mom says. *He can get his family through a New York blizzard.*

They arrive safely at the conference center.
Her mother minds the baby while Vera speaks
from the podium. After some applause, she hurries out
to see how her boy is faring.

The next day her speech is reported
on the front page of the *Washington Post:*
YOUNG MOTHER FINDS CENTER OF CREATION.

The Promise
WASHINGTON, DC

Vera and Bob move to the city where she grew up.
Bob takes a job doing math and physics research.
By the time their firstborn wobbles while learning
to walk, they expect another baby.

Vera brings David to play with her old friend Jane's
two small children. After they help them stack blocks,
arranging a home for a toy bear
and a hangar for tiny airplanes,
Vera quietly asks Jane, *Do you ever get bored?*

Who could ask for more than healthy children?
Seeing Vera's forehead wrinkle, she adds,
I didn't like college as much as you did.
Math was a lot harder than what we did in high school.

I got lost in some of my first classes, Vera says.

But you weren't there to say, "Keep going." No one was.
More than one teacher said,
"Didn't you learn this in high school?"

making it sound like I'd never catch up.
Ow! A child trips over a toy truck, wails.

Back home, Vera settles David for a nap,
makes tea, shoves aside clean but unfolded diapers,
a windup duck, a toy tractor. She picks up
the Astrophysical Journal and flips through pages
to an article about the structure of galaxies.
Her face is tear-blotched when Bob comes home.
He asks, *Didn't you have a good time with Jane?*

Yes. No. Bob, I'm not an astronomer. I need a PhD.

He lifts her dark hair, kisses her neck, says, *I took the job*
in Washington knowing there are universities nearby.

The Window

After the Rubins' second child is born,
Vera's mother cares for David and baby Judy
while Vera takes classes at Georgetown University.
She earns a PhD, then teaches physics and math part-time.
One night she walks past the kitchen
where Bob washes dishes
and the room they've made ready for the third baby.
She sits on her daughter's bed and reads her a book
about a lost puppy. After saying, *The end,*
she asks, *Want me to open the window?*

Yes, Mommy. Can I touch the stars?

Nobody can, but you can reach. Vera kisses Judy
and her stuffed rabbit. Then, at the kitchen table,
she moves aside books and cereal boxes with mazes
on the back, tends to calculations until two in the morning.
The work is hard, but it would be harder to set it aside.

Invisible Light

Ten years after Vera gave birth to her first child,
she has her fourth and last baby. The children sleep,
wake, and wonder in a big old house with floors covered
with broken crayons, balsa-wood airplanes,
magnets, experiments, and Tinkertoy skyscrapers.

After David, Judy, Karl, and Allan are all in school,
Vera is hired to do research
at the Carnegie Institution of Science,
which has new equipment that widens horizons.
Kent Ford built a spectroscope that splits visible light
into a spectrum of colors.
It can show evidence of light people can't see,
such as radio or gamma waves, or waves that can warm food,
let doctors see through muscle to bones, or tan skin.

Vera and Kent first study newly discovered quasars,
which are dazzling, wildly energetic, and enormous.
They might contain black holes, also powerful and huge.
Quasars, which are brighter and farther away
than most galaxies,

are a popular subject among astronomers, who usually spend
more time with math and data than observing.
Since Vera's children need her at home,
she'll spend even less time at telescopes than most.
She looks for a focus that scientists will care about,
but not so much they're likely to compete,
or ask a lot of questions before she's certain of answers,
and make her feel like she should rush.

Vera decides to focus on her old interest:
the way stars move in spiral galaxies,
which bulge in the middle with arcing arms.
Her mother takes care of the children when she and Kent
travel to use big telescopes on mountains in Arizona.
Far-off galaxies are easier to see
where there's less atmosphere and light pollution.
Vera's feet and hands are often cold in observatories,
which aren't heated, since telescopes are kept
at the outdoor temperature so they don't distort.

She points the telescope toward stars in Andromeda, M31,
the galaxy nearest to the Milky Way, the galaxy we live in.
Kent attaches the spectrograph, which bends light

the way a prism or a drop of water splinters
into a purple, blue, yellow, and red spectrum.
They take photographs of trails
that sketch shine long after a star's life is over.
Small measurements may lead to big discoveries.

Patterns

Back home, Vera slides photographic plates
under a microscope. She works on calculations
from the thousands of thin lines on the photographs
that stand for a galaxy.
Curving and flat lines show what stars are made of, their size,
temperature, and how far and fast they move.
Starlight moving closer to earth has shorter wavelengths,
shifts to the blue end of the spectrum.
Light that moves away shifts to the red end.

Like a telescope, math pulls in what's grand,
pares in search of what's crucial. She's meticulous.
Minuscule errors matter the way a slight change
in the angle of a wrist can widely shift the arc of a ball struck
by a bat or hockey stick, or tossed into a hoop.
She measures spaces between the strips of colors
to calculate the speed of stars
and the distances between them,
looks for patterns between a star's speed
and its distance from the galaxy's center.
Each answer stirs new questions.

Summer

The family camps out west, where the children
scramble up boulders, shout, play king of the mountain.
At night, stars show off above the soft flicker of campfires.
Vera wants her children to know science is beautiful
both on paper and seen in the sky.
Much can be found in the places where few look.

Inheritance

Come inside, Allan, Vera calls to her youngest child,
who crouches by the steps, breaking open
chunks of granite and quartz. She says, *It's getting dark.*
I don't want you to hammer off a finger.
She walks through the living room, where David
practices the violin. Karl builds a model of a triceratops.
A math book is wedged between sofa cushions. She pulls
it out and flips through. Pictures of pale, freckled boys
with clipped hair are shown measuring boards
and counting nails for a tree house
or mapping ways to outer space.
Girls wearing crisp dresses work on cookie recipes.

Vera heads to Judy's bedroom after hearing her scream.
She finds her daughter hunched over her desk.
Judy pushed aside poems she's written
to make room for an open book under the green lamp.
I hate math. I can't do this!

Vera looks over her equation. *You meant to get it right.*

I don't even care. Math isn't good for anything.

You use math when you write poems or sew.

The sewing machine is broken. Mom, go away.

Vera leaves the door open. She pushes aside
books on the dining room table, copies
of the *Astrophysical Journal* she should sort, saving
those she hasn't read yet or that have articles she wrote.
She hears Bob and Judy by the broken sewing machine
they're taking apart on the kitchen table. She taught
Judy how to lay down a tissue pattern, measure,
with her mouth full of pins. Bob shows her
how gears mesh together, what moves the needle
up and down, what catches and nudges along the cloth.

Paper Skirt
CALTECH, CALIFORNIA, 1965

Vera applies to use the world's biggest telescope.
Palomar Observatory stands on a southern California
mountain whose peak reaches over fog, but not so high
that stars are likely to be hidden in clouds.
Desert, woods, and fern meadows surround the white dome.

Vera receives a typed letter saying: *Due to limited facilities,
it's not possible for the observatory to accept applications
from women.* Penciled in before *not possible* is *usually.*

Vera takes that penciled-in word to mean *Yes.*
She flies across the country, finds the observatory bathroom
has a picture of a man's silhouette on the door.
She cuts out a paper skirt, tapes it on top.
Now there's a ladies' room. That wasn't so hard.

Belief

Vera spends more time searching than with certainty.
Stuck on a problem, she plays a few songs on the piano,
takes a walk, comes back and finds an equation
no longer stubborn, but ready to reveal secrets.
Still trying to understand how galaxies orbit,
Vera sketches. Moving her wrist and gaze together,
she turns what she sees into lines.

She knows that planets closest to the sun move faster
than planets farther from the sun and its gravitational force.
She's been taught that stars within galaxies also move fastest
near the center, dense and brilliant with stars,
and more slowly on the outskirts.
But flat spectral lines suggest the outermost stars
move at the same speed as stars close to the core.
The rotation curve is flat, she tells Kent,
This means the stars on the outer curve
don't slow down because of their distance from the core,
the way most astronomers have long assumed.

Doubt paves a path to discovery.

Could something be wrong with her eyes or mind?
Was she daydreaming, distracted, or tired?
She goes back over stacked pages of math,
looking for a mistake deep in
that might have set everything else astray.
Not one digit is off. She checks the spectroscope
and cameras for flaws in the mechanics
and lenses but finds nothing wrong. She breathes
deeply into the courage to believe what she sees.
Whether on the outskirts of the Andromeda galaxy
or near the center, stars move at the same speed.

The Backyard
JULY 20, 1969

The Rubins' living room smells of butter and popcorn.
The black-and-white television flickers with smoky images
of three astronauts arriving near the moon.
An electric fan hums in the heat. Models of rockets
built by their youngest son are propped among geology books
their oldest brought back from college and college catalogs
ordered by Judy, who will apply for admission in the fall.

As the television shows the lunar module land on the moon,
the whole family cheers and hugs. Then Karl dozes off.
Bob tells eight-year-old Allan, *It's going to be a while*
before the astronauts step out onto the moon.
You might want to catch some sleep.

Allan shakes his head.
His oldest brother stacks, then tips over
books to show how continents shifted. David says,
It happened long ago, before people were around.

Then how do you know it happened? Allan asks.

There's a long valley along undersea mountains
where the break might have been. Now almost all
scientists believe in continental shift, but hardly any
did when Mom and Dad were your age.

Vera talks about the thousands of workers
who helped get three people into space.
Allan slides off the sofa, says, *I want to go outside.*
I know we can't see the astronauts up there,
but I want to look.

Allan, his sister, and his mother go to the backyard.
Televisions in neighbors' houses glow faintly blue.
Allan looks up. *I wish the moon was round and yellow tonight.*

They chose to land when the moon was a crescent,
so the sun will rise over them, Vera says. *The long morning*
shadows will help the astronauts find their way around.

I bet they wish it were brighter, Allan says.
What if they get lost in dark matter?

Dark matter is much farther away, Judy says.
No one can see it.

Then how do you know it's there? he asks.

Nobody knows for sure. For now it's a theory,
an idea with "maybe" in it, Vera says.
A lot of science starts out that way, until someone finds proof.
Our best telescopes can't spot dark matter,
but we might see how it changes what's around it.

I hate dark matter. I like rocks.
Allan sprints back into the house.

I'm afraid there are many who'd agree with him, Vera says.

A lot of people don't like what can't be seen.
But you always root for underdogs.
Judy steps closer to her mother, says,
Maybe I'll study astronomy in college.

There's a lot of math in those classes, Vera says.
I remember when you complained about math every night.

It can be hard. But it's cool when everything
becomes clear, Judy says. *And I have people to help.*

I still need help, but I have different questions.
None of us work alone. Vera touches her shoulder.
I hope you find support in college.
You have more choices of where to go than I did.

Do you think I could get into Princeton? Judy asks.
This year they're admitting women for the first time.

I believe in you. I'll be proud wherever you go.
Vera is still a little angry
that the university rejected her application,
though everything turned out all right. *Now let's go inside*
and see what's happening on the moon.

Portraits

After Judy collects a few college acceptances,
Vera goes with her to tour Princeton University,
which just opened to women. The young tour guide
can't meet female eyes as he leads a group down
corridors decorated with portraits of men.
Their lips look pinched with disapproval,
like those of a man who must be an alumnus
visiting with his son.
He wears a button that says BRING BACK THE OLD PRINCETON.
Apparently enough share the sentiment
for someone to make such buttons. Heading back
to the car, Judy asks,
Mom, will you be disappointed if I don't go here?

No. It's one thing to admit young women,
another to make them feel welcome.
I don't advise anyone to join a department
where there aren't any women professors. Vera pauses.
I'm glad you want to study astronomy. But it can be hard.
Not many people will understand your work.

I feel kind of sorry for them. Don't you? Judy tilts her head.

Discovery

Week after week, month after month, year after year,
Vera looks beyond Andromeda to other spiral galaxies,
measures red shifts and blue shifts, wondering
if the stars in them also move at the same speed.
She looks at twenty more spiral galaxies, forty, then sixty,
star field by star field, including bright and dim galaxies,
and ones with loose or tight spirals.
She determines the speed of star after star after star
as each orbits its galaxy's bright core,
works out the distances, sets numbers on graphs.
The results come out the same,
enough so that she can generalize from her examples.

Why don't the more distant stars slow down?
What keeps them from spinning off into the vast beyond?
Vera believes that's due
to the gravitational pull of dark matter.
Scientists have speculated that dark matter,
which can't be seen, may be shaping the universe,
but no one has found proof it exists. Until now.
Evidence shines from her math.

Two A.M.

Vera wanders past a closet where old sandbox toys
mix with sneakers, rubber boots that probably fit nobody,
hammers, split rocks, a jump rope with silver bells
on the handles, butterfly nets
made from bent coat hangers, sticks, and netting.
In the dining room her collection of old globes
show changes in what's known of earth and sky.

It's two o'clock in the morning, but she goes upstairs
and wakes up Bob. He's more handsome than ever
with silver streaking his black hair. She says,
I found evidence of dark matter.
Enough to publish and persuade skeptics.

I always believed. Bob throws back the covers.
What has it been, fifteen years of work?
What kind of celebration can measure up to that?

None. That's why one had better love her work.
Bob gets out of bed, heads to the kitchen,
takes a tub of ice cream from the freezer and two spoons

from a cluttered drawer. Vera turns off all the lights.
They sit on the porch steps,
eating while looking up at the sky.
After all those years of long late nights,
she understands that most of the universe
is made of dark matter. Most of the universe is unknown.
Like the necessary pulse between notes of music,
the darkness between stars is as important as the stars.

Mother and Daughter
AMHERST, MASSACHUSETTS, 1986

Vera visits Judy, who just won an award
for teaching in the astronomy department
at the University of Massachusetts.
After Judy puts her young daughter to bed,
she asks Vera about the response to her discovery.

Flat lines show up in galaxy after galaxy, so not many argue
with the evidence, Vera says. But some find it hard to believe
that darkness between stars has a force.
Now tell me about your work.

Judy describes her research on how stars form
in spiral galaxies. She reminisces about college,
when she studied with the three other women
in her physics class. *One night we talked about growing up*
and realized that all of us had fathers who were physicists.
I was the only one whose mother also loved math and science.
But the point is, girls shouldn't have to have relatives
in the field to be encouraged. Too many girls still drop out.

I often thought my old friend Jane would have been happier
if she'd kept on with math. When people ask me
how I worked past the discouragement, I say they should ask
women like Jane, who couldn't. I was lucky, but . . .

Mom, you weren't just lucky. I remember
you talking about that high school teacher
who told you to stay away from science
and that advice to make a career in astronomical painting.

We have to just laugh off some things, Vera says.

In my freshman seminar, the professor asked me to make the tea.
That garbage still goes on, and not everybody can ignore it.
Mom, you showed the existence of dark matter!
Where's your Nobel Prize? I know not everyone
can win, but it would make a difference
if more women were on awards committees.
When are you going to talk about that in public?

I don't want to discourage any girl from science.

I know. But unfair things happen.
And we need to know we're not alone.

The Front Door

Vera gives talks at universities and at the Cosmos Club
in Washington, DC, where gentlemen distinguished
in art, literature, science, or public service gather.
When told women must enter the private club
through the side door, Vera catches her breath,
but walks to her place behind the podium. She explains
how dark matter makes up much of the universe,
but no one knows what it is. It could be made of stars
not big enough to shine or particles smaller than atoms.
It might hold clues to entirely new dimensions of time
and space, hint at an expanding universe.

She looks at the audience entirely of men and speaks
of Maria Mitchell, who was inspired by Caroline Herschel,
the first and so far the only woman to win
a gold medal from the Royal Astronomical Society.
She praises Maud Makemson, her former professor,
who did astronomical calculations for the moon launch.
Some women work without being paid. Imagine
all the progress that could be made in math and science
if we were encouraged instead of held back.

After the crowd leaves, the club president says,
We hope you'll talk here again.

Thank you, she replies. *If I come back,*
I'll use the front door.

Now and Then

New telescopes are flown far into space
so more can be seen without the atmosphere in the way.
The farther Vera looks, the further she sees back in time.
Most observatories are now heated.
Vera doesn't have to change the signs on restrooms.
She saves time working on computers
instead of calculating using slower machines,
and she no longer must wait
for photographs to develop in a basin of chemicals.

She compiles the first catalog of dark nebulae,
which are the birthplaces of stars and planets,
and makes a new discovery: stars in a galaxy
don't all rotate in the same direction.
Answers open more questions
she may explore for the rest of her life.

Darkness Is a Door

The universe is not just what we see but what we can't see.
In recognition of Vera Rubin's work
analyzing spectra of more than two hundred galaxies,
showing how most matter is invisible and mysterious,
the Royal Astronomical Society gives her a gold medal.
She's thankful but believes another century and a half
shouldn't pass before a third woman receives that gold.

She writes letters and gives talks protesting
all-male meetings, conferences, or college departments.
Common conversations matter too.
Vera continues her work at the Carnegie Institution,
but when she travels to give speeches,
she invites graduate students from across the country
to have a cup of coffee. She asks
an assistant professor, *How is your research going?*
The young woman says, *In all the years I've worked,*
no one ever asked for my professional opinion.

Young women confide about men who took credit
for their research. One says that she was denied a job

when a man said she was too pretty for him to concentrate
with her nearby. Some speak about men who touch them
in ways they don't like or pursue them with words
after they've told them to stop.
Women report harassment to authorities who advise them
to ignore interruptions or make light of creepy invitations.
Some department heads hint that the men's work
is more important than a woman scientist's sense of safety.

It shouldn't be our job to stand up to these men,
but if we don't, one day we may find we don't want
to go back to work, Vera tells a student.
There are too many ways to make a woman
feel as if she doesn't belong. Vera says,
Learn about women who made a difference.
Everyone should know about Caroline Herschel.
Everyone should know Florence Nightingale, Hertha Ayrton,
Marie Tharp, Katherine Johnson, Edna Lee Paisano,
and more. Like the important darkness
between stars, every name matters.

Winter Solstice

JACKSON HOLE, WYOMING, 1996

Vera steps outside a cabin far from city lights
that scrub out darkness. The valley is lovely
in summer, with the scent of sagebrush
and the ripple and rush of an unfrozen river.
Vera prefers to be here now, when December nights,
filled with questions and answers, last long.

She stands under the bright-speckled spill of nebulae,
where new stars come to be. Looking across snow
to a canyon, she can faintly hear her grandchildren
playing board games by firelight with her grown children:
two geologists, one mathematician, and an astronomer.

A granddaughter bursts from the cabin,
looking unsteady in her snow gear. *Wait for me!*
Her last word echoes from the canyon.
As she gets close, she asks, *Where were you?*
Daddy said you're counting stars. I can help.
I even know double digits.

Vera picks up the little girl. Her hair smells like woodsmoke. The child asks, *How many stars are there?*

In our galaxy? Vera replies. *Billions.*
And there are billions of galaxies in the universe.

Have you seen them all?

Not even close. Above, underfoot, and all around them, wonders wait to be discovered.

BEHIND THE VERSE
A NOTE FROM THE AUTHOR

Grasping Mysteries honors women who used math to frame and solve problems, fix things, or understand the size of the universe. Women have done groundbreaking work in pure mathematics, but here I chose to show ways math shapes other fields. Too many girls who want to make changes in medicine or the environment, for instance, are stopped by their lack of confidence in math. Not all science depends on measurements and equations, but much does, and a command of math will make anyone more independent. From the time girls first stack wooden blocks, toss a stick to a dog, climb a tree, sew, knit, bead, cook, balance on a beam, or bandage an arm or a wing, they should know of the many ways math marks the world. They deserve to be told: *I believe in you.* Sometimes that message comes from history.

Keeping in mind real discoveries and dates, I imagined

scenes with dialogue and sensory detail based on what's known about the time, place, and questions of girls who loved math. I wanted to show not just the grand moments of discovery, but the importance of what's not always recorded. History can happen when no one watches, as simply as a girl wonders about the sea, looks at the sky, counts backward, turns over a rock, or reaches up holding the string of a kite.

All the women in this book faced discouragement. None let insults or a lack of faith stop them. With care and curiosity, they did astonishing work. They believed change is possible on earth and far above. More secrets of the universe are certain to be found.

WOMEN WHO
WIDENED HORIZONS

✦

CAROLINE HERSCHEL (1750–1848) endured sickness and loneliness throughout her childhood. She grew happier when her older brother, William, invited her to live and work with him in England. He tutored her in mathematics so she could help him organize his observations of stars, and then she read upper-level math books on her own. Caroline was the first woman in the world to discover a comet and have it named after her. At a time when most women who earned money did so for domestic work such as cooking or cleaning, Caroline Herschel became the first woman to be paid for work in science and math. Scanning the sky for forty years, she discovered eight comets. She was the first woman to receive a gold medal from the Royal Astronomical Society. Her *Catalog of Nebulae and Clusters of Stars* is still used today.

FLORENCE NIGHTINGALE (1820–1910) grew up in a mansion where her father taught her mathematics. After her knowledge surpassed his, he bought her books. Florence broke through the expectations of her family and society to become a nurse at a time when caring for the sick or injured in hospitals was done mostly by men. Today, she is primarily remembered as a kind and wise nurse, but after leaving the military hospital at the end of the Crimean War, Florence Nightingale spent many more years at home organizing health records and developing charts that would lead to social change. She helped start a nursing school in London, the first one not run by a religious order. She was one of the founders of medical statistics and was known for developing polar area diagrams, sometimes called rose diagrams or coxcomb charts.

HERTHA MARKS AYRTON (1854–1923) loved watching her father fix watches when she was young. Wanting to know how things worked was the force behind her education. She registered twenty-six patents for her inventions, which included mathematical dividers and devices related to her work on arc lights and the propulsion of air. (I found no record of whether Hertha ever discussed patents with her friend Marie Curie, who refused to take out patents on discoveries she made, believing that science should profit not just one person, but all.) Hertha Ayrton was called the first female electrical engineer, and her book *The Electric Arc*, published in 1902, remains in print. She was always inventive, but in her later years, she spent more time fighting for women's rights. After her death, her friend Ottilie Blind endowed the Hertha Ayrton Research Fellowship at their alma mater, Girton College. Hertha's daughter, Barbara Ayrton-Gould, became a member of Parliament in 1945.

MARIE THARP (1920–2006) loved joining her father in fields, where he took measurements for government maps. His job meant the family had to move almost every year, so Marie's closest relationships were with her parents, who encouraged her to be independent and curious. She loved learning about all aspects of mathematics, but chose a career that involved moving figures taken from real places onto charts and maps. Marie Tharp and Bruce Heezen created the first map of the entire ocean floor. The World Ocean Floor Panorama not only helped scientists understand what's under the water that covers more than two-thirds of the earth, but suggests how the continents shifted. In 2009 the Marie Tharp Historical Map was added to Google Earth. The unknown parts of the ocean are shown as blurry on the map to suggest what's still left to discover.

KATHERINE JOHNSON (1918–2020) loved to figure out math problems, even before she started school. There, she excelled in all subjects and stayed at the top of her class through graduate school, which she left after becoming pregnant with the first of her three daughters. After taking a job at NASA, she calculated trajectories, launch windows, and emergency plans for missions to put Americans in space and on the moon. She made plans for flights to Mars. Many of her honors came after the end of her remarkable career. NASA gave her five Special Achievement Awards and named a research building after her. The Oscar-nominated movie *Hidden Figures* was partially based on her life, and highlighted the time when astronaut John Glenn was scheduled to be the first American to orbit Earth but asked that Katherine Johnson first check the math. She worked swiftly, calculating to two decimal points beyond what the computer did. In 2015 she was awarded the Presidential Medal of Freedom.

EDNA LEE PAISANO (1948–2014) loved mathematics and the plains and canyons where she grew up. Because she wasn't sure how math could help her give back to the Nez Perce Nation, she earned an advanced degree in social work. Working in schools, she encouraged children to play with blocks, thus learning to love addition, subtraction, and division. When rheumatoid arthritis made it increasingly painful for her to sit on floors or crouch by little chairs, Edna Lee Paisano took a job in Washington, DC. As the first Native American to work full-time for the United States Census Bureau, she worked with sets and subsets to compare the needs of young people in various places, factoring in the ways that hunger and uncertainty might affect anyone's ability to pay attention. As a supervisor, she developed a more inclusive census program, evaluated and interpreted data, researched administrative records for tribal governments, conducted workshops, and prepared testimonies for Congress. During her twenty-year career at the Census Bureau, she oversaw a large increase in the representation of American Indians and Alaskan Natives.

VERA RUBIN (1928–2016) grew up asking lots of questions. Her interests were encouraged by her father, an electrical engineer who helped her build a telescope in the backyard of their Washington, DC, home, during a time shortly before light pollution in the city made it difficult to see stars. Although she was told that girls couldn't study astronomy, she earned a degree in the subject at Vassar College, then went on to earn a PhD at Georgetown University. She studied more than two hundred galaxies during her career and proved the existence of dark matter. Vera Rubin was elected to the National Academy of Sciences and won the National Medal of Science, the most prestigious award for science in the United States. She used the recognition of her work to help other women who loved math and science feel confident in workplaces that were too often unfriendly. In 1996 she became the second woman to win the gold medal of the Royal Astronomical Society. An area of Mars is named the Vera Rubin Ridge, and a small planet is named Asteroid 5726 Rubin in her honor.

SELECTED BIBLIOGRAPHY

Books noted with * were written for young readers.

✶ CAROLINE HERSCHEL ✶

Caroline Herschel has never entirely vanished from the history of science, but her role as a devoted sister often has been more emphasized than her work charting celestial orbits. Caroline's letters and journals remain in print, with many thanks due to Michael Hoskin, who has written much about the extraordinary Herschel family, including the two books listed here.

* Armstrong, Mabel. *Women Astronomers: Reaching for the Stars*. Marcola, Oregon: Stone Pine Press, c2008.

———. *Caroline Herschel: Priestess of the New Heavens*. Sagamore Beach: Science History Publications/USA, 2013.

Hoskin, Michael A. *Discoverers of the Universe: William and Caroline Herschel*. Princeton, New Jersey: Princeton University Press, c2011.

* McCully, Emily Arnold. *Caroline's Comets: A True Story*. New York: Holiday House, 2017.

Osen, Lynn. M., *Women in Mathematics*. Cambridge, MA: MIT Press, 1974.

* Venkatraman, Padma. *Double Stars: The Story of Caroline Herschel*. Greensboro, NC, Morgan Reynolds Publishing, c2007.

Winterburn, Emily. *The Quiet Revolution of Caroline Herschel: The Lost Heroine of Astronomy*. Stroud, UK: The History Press, 2017.

✳ HERTHA AYRTON ✳

The memoir written by Evelyn Sharp, who was a friend of Hertha Ayrton's daughter, Barbara Ayrton-Gould, was my main source on their lives. I also read Hertha's scientific book about arc lights, some about the history of electric lights, and the movements in England to promote female education and the vote. Some books about Hertha's friend, the prize-winning physicist Marie Curie, also provided information about women in science in the early twentieth century.

Jones, Claire G. *Femininity, Mathematics, and Science, 1880–1914*. New York: Palgrave Macmillan, 2009.

Sharp, Evelyn. *Hertha Ayrton: A Memoir*. London: Edward Arnold & Co., 1926.

Swaby, Rachel. *Headstrong: 52 Women Who Changed Science—and the World*. New York: Broadway Books, 2015.

✴ FLORENCE NIGHTINGALE ✴

Of all the women in this book, the most has been written about Florence Nightingale. She was famous in her day, had a funeral that filled London streets, and has remained in the public eye, with many nurses reciting a pledge that honors her goals. Most of her fame is due to the way Florence opened the nursing profession to women and emphasized humane care in hospitals. I focused on the way that mathematics shaped her life and work. Also, having long heard Florence being called "the Lady with the Lamp," I could not resist reporting the story of why she was also less famously called "the Lady with the Hammer." While she brought compassion to medical care, it took strength, grit, and mathematics to enact her reforms.

Gill, Gillian. *Nightingales: The Extraordinary Upbringing and Curious Life of Miss Florence Nightingale.* New York: Random House, 2004.

* Gorrell, Gina K. *Heart and Soul: The Story of Florence Nightingale.* Toronto, Canada: Tundra Books, 2000.

* Noyce, Pendred E. *Magnificent Minds: 16 Pioneering Women in Science and Medicine.* Boston, MA: Tumblehome Learning, 2015.

* Reef, Catherine. *Florence Nightingale: The Courageous Life of the Legendary Nurse.* New York: Houghton Mifflin Harcourt, 2016.

✶ MARIE THARP ✶

The biography *Soundings*, by Hali Felt, was my main source of information on Marie Tharp. I also looked at professional articles, and the book Marie wrote with colleagues, to get a sense of the shape of her work.

Marie Tharp did most of her ocean studies before women were allowed on a government research ship. Title IX changed that restriction. Evelyn J. Fields, who graduated college with a math degree in 1971, became the first woman to work for the National Oceanic and Atmospheric Administration, and years later the first woman and first African American to hold the position of NOAA rear admiral.

While Evelyn helped collect data in the Atlantic, Pacific, Caribbean, and Alaskan waters, much of the ocean, which covers almost three-quarters of Earth, remains unmapped. Stories also are yet to be known of the many women of color who work doing math and science in the uniformed services.

* Burleigh, Robert. *Solving the Puzzle Under the Sea: Marie Tharp Maps the Ocean Floor*. New York: Simon & Schuster, 2016.

Felt, Hali. *Soundings: The Story of the Remarkable Woman Who Mapped the Ocean Floor.* New York: Henry Holt and Co., 2012.

*Lawlor, Laurie. *Super Women: Six Scientists Who Changed the World.* New York: Holiday House, 2017.

✦ KATHERINE JOHNSON ✦

Those of us who write these days about Katherine Johnson owe a big debt to Margot Lee Shetterly, whose books about Katherine, and other "hidden figures" who worked for NASA, reveal an inspiring history. I read and listened to interviews posted online, and articles about civil rights and space exploration, to understand some of what this brave mathematician faced at school and work.

* Becker, Helaine. *Counting on Katherine: How Katherine Johnson Saved Apollo 13*. New York: Henry Holt and Co., 2018.

* Cline-Ransome, Lesa. *Counting the Stars: The Story of Katherine Johnson, NASA Mathematician*. New York: Simon & Schuster, 2019.

* Slade, Suzanne. *A Computer Called Katherine: How Katherine Johnson Helped Put America on the Moon*. New York: Little Brown Books and Company, 2019.

* Johnson, Katherine G. *Reaching for the Moon: The Autobiography of NASA Mathematician Katherine Johnson*. New York: Simon & Schuster, 2019.

Shetterly, Margot Lee. *Hidden Figures: The American Dream and the Untold Story of the Black Women Mathematicians Who Helped Win the Space Race*. New York: William Morrow, 2016.

* ———. *Hidden Figures: Young Readers' Edition*. New York: HarperCollins, 2016.

* Shetterly, Margot Lee, and Winifred Conkling. *Hidden Figures: The True Story of Four Black Women and the Space Race*. New York: HarperCollins, 2018.

Warren, Wini. *Black Women Scientists in the United States*. Bloomington: Indiana University Press, c1999.

Williams, Talithia. *Power in Numbers: The Rebel Women of Mathematics*. New York: Race Point Publishing, 2018.

✴ EDNA LEE PAISANO ✴

The sections in the books noted here are precious, but most other information about Edna Lee Paisano is online, and often about rather technical details of her work. As I did with all the women here, I read about where she grew up and worked, letting the places she loved suggest her values. I studied pictures of goods, like those Edna sold with her grandmother as a girl on Nez Perce land, noting the math, as well as the art, that's needed in beading and weaving. Both math and poetry are shaped by patterns, so I wanted Edna's work in statistics to echo the themes in the section about Florence Nightingale, despite the other differences of their lives. In 2022, the NSF Vera C. Rubin Observatory will open in Cerro Pachón, Chile, as the first observatory operated by the United States to be named after a woman.

Perl, Teri. *Women and Numbers: Lives of Women Mathematicians Plus Discovery Activities*. San Carlos, CA: Wide World Publishing, c1993.

Sterrett, Andrew, ed. *101 Careers in Mathematics*. 3rd ed. Rhode Island: American Mathematical Society, 2014.

✴ VERA RUBIN ✴

Reading the *New York Times* obituary of Vera Rubin made me wonder: Why haven't I heard about this scientist? That question is often the origin of my writing. Vera became the second woman, after Caroline Herschel, to win the Gold Medal of the Royal Astronomical Society, which reflects how much needs to change for math- and science-loving women, as well as what *has* changed. While Caroline's work was built upon the way she could help her brother, Vera's life shows that a woman with a good husband can raise four children and do path-breaking work.

I read online interviews and Vera's collected essays and speeches in a book I borrowed from the Science and Engineering Library at the University of Massachusetts. Some I read while sitting on the edge of the campus near a sun wheel—a circle of stones that shows changes in the sky—made under the direction of Vera's daughter, Judy Young, who was a professor in the astronomy department.

Ambrose, Susan A., et al. *Journeys of Women in Science and Engineering: No Universal Constants*. Philadelphia: Temple University Press, 1997.

Clinton, Hillary Rodham, and Chelsea Clinton. *The Book of Gutsy Women: Favorite Stories of Courage and Resilience*. New York: Simon & Schuster, 2019.

*Ignotofsky, Rachel. *Women in Science: 50 Fearless Pioneers Who Changed the World*. New York: Ten Speed Press, 2016.

Lightman, Alan P., and Roberta Brawer. *Origins: The Lives and Worlds of Modern Cosmologists*. MA: Harvard University Press, 1990.

Rubin, Vera C. *Bright Galaxies, Dark Matters*. New York: American Institute of Physics, c1997.

* Stille, Darlene R. *Extraordinary Women Scientists*. Chicago: Childrens Press, c1995.